HE SAID SHE SAID

jacob
&
lily

Shannon Layne

EPIC
Press

Jacob & Lily
He Said She Said: Book #2

Written by Shannon Layne

Copyright © 2016 by Abdo Consulting Group, Inc.

Published by EPIC Press™
PO Box 398166
Minneapolis, MN 55439

Cover design and illustration by Candice Keimig
Edited by Marianna Baer

LIBRARY OF CONGRESS CATALOGING-IN-PUBLICATION DATA

Layne, Shannon.
Jacob & Lily / Shannon Layne.
p. cm. — (He said, she said)
Summary: When Lily starts talking to Jacob in a chat room online, secrets come
flooding out, yet she has no idea of his real identity. And as they open up to each
other more and more, they're both left with the choice to leave everything the same
as it's always been, or to take the leap that would change both of them forever.
ISBN 978-1-68076-036-1 (hardcover)
1. Online dating—Fiction. 2. Interpersonal relations—Fiction. 3. High school
students—Fiction. 4. Young adult fiction. I. Title.
[Fic]—dc23
2015932724

EPICPRESS.COM

"You know what happens when you dream of falling? Sometimes you wake up. Sometimes the fall kills you. And sometimes, when you fall, you fly."
— Neil Gaiman
The Sandman, Vol. 6: Fables and Reflections

lily

My mother was a dancer. She traveled all over the world with companies, performing every night in a new city. She wore leotards that sparkled when she spun in the spotlight and headpieces made of feathers and crystals. She was light on her feet, a concoction of silk and steel tendons that bore her weight on impossibly extended limbs. She was used to this, to the sweat and blood and work, but also to people's eyes following her across a stage, watching the way her body moved. She met my father when she was performing in Paris. His eyes were the only ones she could pick out in the darkness of the audience, she said, like a candle's flame in the night.

When he was allowed backstage she was sitting in her private room, already dressed, and waiting for him. He followed her back to the United States.

She never would have stopped, I don't think, if she hadn't gotten pregnant with me.

We have a photo that was taken the night I was born. My mother is red-faced, sweating, but instead of an expression of joy or love on her face there is only unwilling resignation. She blamed me for needing her body so badly that it took away all possibility of her dancing again. The pregnancy had been difficult for her; carrying me put more strain on her back and her knees, which had already been pushed to the breaking point by the life she'd chosen as a ballerina. An old back injury had flared up again so badly during the pregnancy that, even without me to take care of, she didn't know if her body could stand up to the strain any longer.

I think she would have preferred if I looked nothing like her, that I'd take after my father's side of the family.

None of my mother's plans worked out too well.

I have my father's black hair and cobalt eyes, but every bone in my face mirrors my mother. She may be blonde and light-eyed but we look like twins. I'm shorter than her by a hairsbreadth, with the same long legs and slim hips. She looks at me and sees who she once was, eighteen years ago, when the world lay at her feet.

She prayed I would be born without the burning she had inside her—without her drive or talent. But I was a natural in my ballet slippers when I could barely walk. I advanced to pointe and my feet hardened and my body adapted as though I were born to it. And in a way, I guess I was. I stole her dream without meaning to, without plan or plot, the way the sunrise steals the dark heart of the moon at the end of each night.

jacob

My dad started taking me on camping trips when I was almost too small to carry my own backpack. We'd hike for days, through forests and across rivers even he didn't know the names of. On the third day of one of our adventures, we turned a corner to come face to face with a mountain lion. I remember the way the bead of sweat trickled down the back of my neck, the way I tried to move my feet, which felt as if they'd grown roots. She was tawny and lithe, with massive paws, and her eyes were cool and yellow, like melted butter. She studied me for ten long seconds, her moon-eyes delving into me, and then she flicked her tail and disappeared into the brush. I'll never forget the way her yellow eyes burned into me. I thought, for a moment, that she could see right through my skin to where my heart pounded inside.

My dad grew up in a small town east of Omak, Washington, and he always said the name of the town in a way that was impossible to pronounce—the original name given to it by the Native Americans who had populated the area before the white man ever knew it existed. I still can't say it right. My mom was from Bellingham; they met at college in Olympia and moved to Seattle when they had me.

"Your father wasn't the most romantic type," my mom would say. "He had barely spoken a word to me until the very day he asked me out."

"We had a class together," said my dad. "Animal Biology. Your mom knew the answer to every question. Her hand was always in the air. She'd come to class after the gym, wearing these workout pants—"

"That's enough, John."

My dad would wink at me and wrap my mom in a bear hug until they both toppled onto the couch. We've had the same couch for as long as I can remember—soft and worn, sagging a little in the middle. The broken chair, though, my mom donated to my basement collection. The basement is the one room in the house that's completely my own.

My mom got pregnant with the twins as a "surprise" gift they announced to me three days after my twelfth birthday. Elaina and Elizabeth are six now, obsessed with Taylor Swift, and essentially a huge pain in my ass. My parents helped re-do the basement and I moved out of my room to make room for the girls. Now, the basement is filled with everything a guy could need, like old beanbag chairs and a mini-fridge. There's a set of weights, too, because I figured a nerd like me couldn't be nerdy *and* skinny if he wanted to survive high school.

That's where I saw her for the first time. On our very first day, standing on the stone steps of Henry James High School, in front of the crumbling brick. I don't know why I remember such an insignificant moment so well. She was already centered within a group of laughing and talking people, all craving her attention. She had dark hair that shone like a raven's wing in the hallway lights and I could tell she wanted to be anywhere else. I watched as she laughed and smiled and pretended, but I could tell. As I watched her look around, dark eyes flashing over familiar faces, something came over me not unlike the meeting with the wild cat so many years ago. The fangs and fur were missing, but there was the same powerful gaze, the same way I felt like I was being studied by something untamable and wild. She only looked at me for a second, but I felt it. I knew she was looking for something she didn't know she needed.

I wouldn't know until years later that it was me.

CHAPTER 1
lily

"**M**ove, move, move," I mumble to myself, trying to maneuver through the knot of traffic in front of my high school. It's seven thirty-four in the evening, and Rob hates when I'm late. Baseball practice is just ending. School might be out in another week or so, but Rob's summer league is just beginning, and they'll play in tournaments throughout the summer. I twist around a truck awkwardly stuck in the middle of the parking lot and aim for the spot closest to the cages, where Rob likes me to park. I check my watch and open and close my hands over and over on the steering wheel. Lately the prospect of seeing Rob has made me more anxious than happy. I'm leaving at the end of summer, though—he knows that. We both know that in the long run this thing isn't really going anywhere.

Rob throws open the door and slides inside, slamming it behind him. He is tall and muscular and looks squished in the front seat of my little Jetta. His hair is light and curls in perfect waves, framing a face with a strong jawline and bright blue eyes that make other girls sigh and giggle in the hallways.

"You're late," he says quietly, and a little part of me quails. I immediately thrust my shoulders back against the completely irrational fear.

"I'm sorry," I say, driving out of the lot. "There was traffic."

"It's fine," says Rob, smiling at me, and I smile in relief.

"I like your hair up like this," he says, threading his fingers up the back of my neck and into the hair that's still twisted into a tight bun from ballet. "You should wear it this way more often."

I bristle under his thinly veiled command. I've always been oversensitive to being told what to do. I think it's a trait I inherited from my mother.

"I wear it this way all the time for ballet," I answer. "I like to have it down when I can."

He doesn't say anything, just spreads his hand around the back of my neck so his fingertips nearly close over my throat. When I glance over at him, he just smiles.

Rob's room is filled with old sports trophies from wrestling and basketball. There are sports pennants, too, and a huge bed with black sheets. We're sitting on it after his practice, the TV turned to—you guessed it—a sports game. I sigh, leaning back on the pillows and crossing my ankles on the bed. It's not even that I'm not into sports—I am, in moderation. But after endless nights of nothing but ESPN, I'm ready for something else. I tap my fingers on my leg, scanning Rob's room. There is a picture of us at prom on his nightstand. He cuts an impressive figure in his black tuxedo, his hair slicked back. I am a glittering shadow in a black dress with long sleeves. I'm turned toward Rob in the photo, whose hand rests on the small of my back. If you look closely enough, you can see his fingers digging into my skin.

Rob treated me like a princess, in the beginning. I could hardly believe the affection and devotion he swamped me with. He carried my books to every class; he rubbed my feet every night after my dance classes; he touched me constantly in public, kissing my head or holding my hand, and I loved the attention. I'd never had anyone lavish it on me the way he did. My dance instructors scrutinized my every move at my private lessons, and my mother saw me every single day, but no one watched every step I took like Rob. It was so romantic that I was completely swept away for a while. Now, I feel like I'm falling deeper and deeper into quicksand that I stepped into willingly.

"Did you read the chapter for Kausen's class?" I ask Rob, who is still focused on the TV.

"Huh?" His eyes manage to tear away from the screen to glance at me, his brow furrowed.

"Chapter 12. *Anna Karenina.* We're supposed to have read it by tomorrow."

Rob just scoffs and turns back to the game.

"I can just have Nick tell me what happens."

"I could tell you what happens."

Rob laughs out loud.

"There's no way you've gotten that far already. That book is so freaking long."

I could tell him that I've read *Anna Karenina* cover to cover at least three times, but I don't. What's the point? I don't need his praise to make me feel smart. I *am* smart, no matter what he says. But I'm also so goddamn bored in this relationship that I'm starting to forget all the reasons I got together with him in the first place.

"Alright, well, I'm going to leave."

I stand up, easing my weight onto muscles that are starting to stiffen. Tonight I had back-to-back practices, which always makes me a little sore.

My mom thinks I should focus on one form of

dance, like jazz or tap or ballet, but I like to incorporate a little of everything. I'm getting more and more into my modern dance classes; they're full of variety and innovation. Ballet is technical and precise. It's my first love, but my tastes are evolving. The annual showcase put on by my studio is coming up soon and I need my routine to be incredible. I'm eighteen now, old enough to be hired by a company to dance professionally. There will be scouts at the showcase, and if they like me, that could mean a job offer.

"You're going already?"

Rob stands up, finally, and blocks the doorway. I eye him from where I'm bending over to grab my bag and my keys.

"Yeah," I say. "I've got stuff to do before bed. And we have school in the morning."

"Maybe you should stay a little longer," he says, taking a step toward me. He leans down and kisses me, his arms circling my waist. Three months ago I would've felt nothing but the thrill of his touch. Now, I'm numb. He kicks the door shut with his foot and nudges me toward the bed with his body until I fall back with a soft thump. He leans over me, still kissing me, and his hands dip under my shirt. I'm still relaxed, not totally unwilling, just a little bored, until his hands start to attempt to roam underneath my sports bra. I twist away because this is a conversation we've had too many times.

"Quit it," I say sharply. I hop off the bed and start toward the door when Rob's hand snakes around my wrist.

"What's the big deal?" says Rob. He tugs on my wrist so I am facing him where he is sitting on the bed.

"We've talked about this. I'm not ready."

"What can I do to help you get there?"

He tugs me to him and nuzzles my earlobe, kissing my neck tenderly, and for a moment, I remember all the reasons I'm with Rob. He can be so sweet and funny and charismatic. I lift his face and kiss him back, my hands on his shoulders, before I pull away.

"I really have to go," I say, my forehead against his.

He gets that mulish look on his face that I dread.

"Fine," he says. "But this can't go on forever, Lily."

I bristle, and he stands, and it looks like we're about to enter into one of our screaming matches that have lately become more and more frequent. But then he looms above me, blocking the door, and all I want is to be home and away from him. So I smile sweetly and nod, and he moves so I can grab my things and leave.

Outside, I take a deep breath and shake my shoulders before climbing back into my car, relieved to be free.

What are you doing with him, Lily?

The question resonates in my mind as I drive away.

I know Rob can be rude and kind of ignorant about things, like literature and well, everything. But I still remember how safe he made me feel, and that's something I've been craving for most of my life.

When my father died, my mom and I were completely on our own. His parents were back in Europe; my mother's were both dead. I was ten years old and we were living in California at the time. I still remember the look on my mom's face for the year or so after he died—pinched and pale, her fear hidden just beneath the surface. We moved around until eventually we wound up in Seattle, with her working as a paralegal. She met my stepdad there, at the firm.

I take a left turn and head toward Queen Anne Hill. I like my stepdad, for the most part. He and I came to a truce, of sorts, after they married. I was a nightmare to him for a while. I refused to speak when he was around, turned up my nose at any little toy or candy he got for me. I'd scream and scream when he came into the house to pick my mother up for a date. When she made it clear that they were getting married and that there wasn't anything I could do about it, I gave in to the entire thing, because I was terrified she'd disappear the way my father did. That's a terror that never really goes away after a person you love leaves you—the overwhelming fear that someone else will leave you behind.

I pull up to the house and shut my car off before reaching for my backpack. I tug at the strap and it immediately flops over, spilling its contents into my backseat.

"Shit," I mutter. I get out and open the back door, balancing on my knees, trying to stuff all my papers and binders back inside. In the process, a notebook slides from the pile I've gathered and onto the seat. As I go to grab it, I pause, flipping it over in my hands. It's not a notebook, not really. It's slick and thin, a gathering of pages that I've been hiding in here for the past month. The comic book is titled *The Adventures of Miss Diamond*. She was the world's first ballerina superhero, written by the person I loved most in the world. She wears an eye mask to protect her identity along with a totally badass black leotard, black bow, even black pointe shoes. On the crown of her head, right in front of her tight bun, there is a sparkling diamond set on a black band.

She was written for me. In the shadow of the car, I trace her dark hair, her thick lashes, and finally the outline of her heart-shaped face, a face that mirrors mine exactly.

CHAPTER 2
jacob

I am re-reading issue No. 18 of Neil Gaiman's series *The Sandman* when I hear a ping from my computer. Full disclosure: my elaborate man cave, AKA basement, is filled with old furniture and a Playstation 3, but also boxes of comic books. My grandpa has a huge attic that the twins always play hide and seek in when we visit, where he keeps boxes and boxes of dusty old comics. I found them one day; my mom and I went up there after we heard Elizabeth screaming because she'd seen a spider, and I ended up going through all of them.

"I remember these," she'd said, pulling the lids off of the boxes. "I used to read these over and over."

"What are they?" I poked my head over her shoulder, and an obsession was born. I took all those old boxes, with my grandpa's permission, and started building a collection of my own. I can't tell you the number of photos my mom has of me and my dad with matching fishing poles, him with a beer in his hand and me with a comic in mine. Elaina even started to get interested when she was learning to read. I started her with *Calvin and Hobbes*, another classic, and she was hooked. Seems like it would be a lot more fun to learn to read with Calvin and his buddy Hobbes than that "Run, Jill, run" bullshit they give you in kindergarten.

The Sandman is my favorite comic series. It was written in the '90s so it's pretty old, but that never bothered me. Morpheus, the main character, always seemed to speak to me on some elemental level. He's this dark, twisted hero who's the king of his own sinister realm of dreams. It's a pretty dark series, and he isn't exactly a bright and shiny character. But as someone who's always felt his dreams were more solid than his reality, he was somewhat of a comfort.

Since I was old enough to be aware of it, I've remembered my dreams. Not just remembered them, though—they stick with me like duct tape, like plastic wrap that you can't get off the tips of your fingers. I'll turn my head during the day and see the flash of a scene from a dream the night before. It was unnerving when I was younger, and it made me obsessive over anything related to nighttime or dreaming. When I found out about *The Sandman* series, which had finished its publication run by the time I was old enough to read, it was incredible. I believed in the King of Dreams and I wished I could be a part of the world he created. Now, I'm old enough to separate myself from the series a little more, and I've found other comics I love. But there's still nothing like it.

I started a club at school called the "Comic-kazes" (clever, right?), and as you would expect, a lot of people thought it was pretty stupid. But there was also a dedicated, albeit small group of people who were interested. We would all go online and chat in public chat rooms with people who were just as devoted as we were about light-hearted subjects most of the time, like Batman versus Spiderman, or whether Venom or the Joker would win in a faceoff. But there were also detailed and serious conversations about the social commentary present in a series like *Preacher,* a series about a small-town preacher who gets possessed by this evil demon and goes looking for God, or what *The Dark Knight Returns* really says about the entire Batman character. So while some people might say we're total nerds (true), some might also say we're educating ourselves in a way that not just encourages and sparks the imagination, but that also provides an opportunity to study the world around us in a critical fashion. I might be the only one I've ever heard say that, but whatever.

At the ping of my computer, I walk over to where my laptop sits on an old desk my mom snagged at a garage sale. I wake up my computer, thinking the noise was an alert from a chat room. I've been idle for a few hours on one of my favorites, a site called Comic Crazies. But I've been waiting to see a certain username come online again.

In the small chat room I created for the Comic-kazes, I know every single person who logs in, most of the time. But on a bigger chat room like Comic Crazies, that isn't always the case. I still recognize the regulars, like me and some of my friends, but there has been one new user handle popping up lately that keeps snagging my attention. When my screen finally brightens I can see that she's back on Comic Crazies, commenting on an old thread someone started a few days ago.

Diamondlily34: my favorite issue is definitely the one where Shakespeare does a cameo…what a plot twist. Morpheus and Shakespeare: dream team

I grin. She—at least I assume she's a she, judging by her user handle—is talking about Sandman, my favorite topic. I type in a quick response and her answering *ping* rapidly greets me. I haven't seen Diamondlily34 much until now. She always makes great comments and she seems to share an appreciation for weird comic characters, like I do. I'm a little curious about her because I recognize all the other handles that stand out to me—except hers. A direct message greets me with another *ping* noise, and I realize it's coming from her handle. My heart beats a little faster, and I stay up late into the night, intoxicated by the words on the screen.

CHAPTER 3
jacob

The last couple days at school I've been a zombie wandering the halls. Mr. Zacharias always has a voice almost guaranteed to put you to sleep but today it seems especially potent. He drones on and on and on about the Socratic method until I start to seriously consider suicide. Since that first night, Diamondlily34 and I have stayed up late, talking about comics. We stayed up until almost two again this morning, but lately something's changed. She's started talking about her personal life, which is totally acceptable, but sort of unusual in the chat room realm. As far as I know, she has no idea who I am. For all she knows I could be a serial killer or a creepy old man. I'm not either of those things, but how is she supposed to know that? And I know nothing about her. I assume she's a girl, but that's about it. She could go to tiny Henry James High School, like me, but who knows? I have no clue. My mind flips back to a message from the night before:

Diamondlily34: *have you ever wished things could be different? that you could see your life under a microscope and just start over?*

Sandman213: *sometimes? i'm not sure tho, not in the way you mean*

Diamondlily34: *yeah*

She'd signed off after that, and I couldn't help thinking that it was something I'd said. I hope she messages me again tonight.

I manage to make it through the rest of the day, somehow. Just as the bell rings and I leave my last class I remember I'm supposed to go pick the girls up today. They're almost out for the summer, just like me, but until they are, Thursday is my day to grab them from elementary school. I sigh, glancing at my watch. If I hurry I should be able to make it before they have to wait too long. I jump down the last few steps and turn the corner toward the parking lot. I don't know if it's my lack of sleep or just plain clumsiness, but without warning I slam into someone on the sidewalk and we both go flying. I stumble a few steps but she actually falls to her knees in the grass next to the cement before catching herself. Everything in her arms drops to the ground and scatters.

"Shit," I say, reaching a hand out for her. "I am so sorry, I wasn't looking—"

"What the hell is your problem?" These words are loud and aggressive, and they come from a hulking man wearing a letterman's jacket, who now looms above me. His brow is furrowed and his eyes are darting from my hand to the face of the girl on the grass, who steps to her feet without my aid. As she brushes grass off her front, I stop breathing. It's Lily Kingston.

We never talk, Lily and I, but I know who she

is. Everyone does. Besides remembering her from the first day of high school, she's in several of my classes. She runs with the crowd that the teachers love—the girls who always get voted into homecoming court and the guys who are all on sports teams. A few of them are actually pretty cool, and I know a few of the girls that are nice, too, but Lily and her boyfriend are the untouchables. It's like there's a barrier of ice surrounding her, although, to be fair to her, I've never spent any time alone with her so I have no idea who she really is. I don't think anyone knows who she really is. But if anyone at this school is close to royalty, it's Lily Kingston.

"There's no problem," I answer. I recognize Rob from every sports team the school has. He's like a walking steroid. "I just didn't see her."

"Rob, it's fine," says Lily, and her voice is like snowflakes.

"Are you hurt at all?" I ask her, and she shakes her head. Rob takes another step toward me, as though he's mad that I spoke to Lily at all. Her eyes are shaded, flicking from Rob to me and back again.

She nudges her hair over her shoulder with the back of her hand and it falls in a sleek black waterfall. It shines almost blue in the sunlight. In the awkwardness of Rob's accusatory stare, I lean down to help Lily gather the papers and the notebook she dropped when I ran into her like the freaking Hulk. In the jumble of papers an image that I recognize snags my attention. It's a black-and-white picture of a ballerina, wearing a black leotard. I only see it for a second before Lily snatches it from my hands, glaring at me. What is it with these people?

"Sorry, again," I say, and I get out of there before someone else can make me feel like an ass. As I leave I can already hear voices rising, Rob's a low rumble and Lily's is a heated hiss. I glance back and she has her hands on her hips and her cheeks are spots of fire. She looks like she can hold her own against anybody. But then I watch Rob's hand come out and snake around her wrist, and she shrinks. I turn away and keep going toward the parking lot; the girls are going to be mad if I'm any later.

CHAPTER 4
jacob

"**Y**ou're late," says Elizabeth, the troublemaker.

"I know," I say. "Sorry, girls."

"It's fine, Jacob," says Elaina. She's always the peacemaker. "Elizabeth's mad because she didn't know the word *ocean* today."

"It doesn't sound like it looks!"

I fight to keep a straight face in the driver's seat, knowing Elizabeth hates being laughed at. She has a serious personality that doesn't react well to teasing. Elaina takes it a little better. I reach back for her toes and she squeals, kicking her legs in the air.

"I'll put a movie on when we get home, okay?"

I say, and both girls nod in their booster seats behind me.

My dad barbecues fish for dinner, one of my favorites, but I pick at it, twirling a piece on my plate over and over with my fork.

"Have you even started to think about packing, Jake?"

My mom is trying to get Elaina to sit down on her chair at the same instant she asks me. The twins have been in the habit lately of standing on their chairs at mealtimes and trying to bend over to eat off of the table. You can imagine the mess. Elizabeth screams and hops off her chair to run out of the room, and my mom sighs. Her hair is in a long braid down her back, the same coffee brown as mine.

"Mom, I'm not leaving for another couple of months," I protest.

I'm going to Vancouver in the fall to study journalism at the university there. I've wanted to write my entire life; it was a natural choice. But I didn't want to go far because of my family and the girls. It sounds kind of stupid, considering I'm eighteen and supposed to want to go to college and get away from my family and all that, but it's not that way at all for me. My dad and I actually hang out on the weekends, fishing or hiking or whatever, and my mom will sketch out ideas for the comics that I come up with. When I was little, my comics were super weird, like my Peanut-Butter-and-Jelly man. He fought crime by sticking his opponents to things with sticky strawberry jam. But she drew out any idea for me, just so I could see what it would look like on paper. I'm no artist, not like she is.

I take my plate to the sink and rinse it off. Elizabeth slides past me in her socks and I snag her around the waist, tickling her until she screams.

"Aren't you starving?" I say. "Look at all this food Dad made for you."

"Fish is gross," says Elaina, who has sidled up next to us. Elizabeth plops into a chair back at the table and Elaina follows suit.

"Not with ketchup," I say, squirting happy faces

onto their plates. Elaina folds her legs and grabs a fork and my mom mouths a "thank you" to me. I finish washing off my plate and head down the stairs to my room.

Something about what happened at school today isn't sitting right with me, and not just because I was forced to interact with a guy like Rob. I have no issue with athletic guys on sports teams in general; a friend of mine from the Comic-kazes, Jason, is on the wrestling team, and I know most of those guys. The issue I have is with people who are assholes, and boyfriends who are assholes to their girlfriends. Whatever, it's not my issue. I don't need to be sticking my nose someplace it doesn't need to be. Some detail is still bothering me about the incident though, and I can't put my finger on what. I change quickly and plug in my earphones before grabbing a pair of weights, thinking a good workout will help take things, take her, off of my mind.

As Lynyrd Skynyrd starts blasting into my ears, I count off reps. Working out clears my mind and burns off energy, and I enjoy it. I'm nowhere close to the size that Rob is, but why would I want to be? The guy is so muscled out that I don't know how he moves at all. My mind flashes back to Lily. Since the first day of high school, I've seen her almost every day. Still, she's never been at the forefront of my mind like this. That's probably because I always assumed our lives were so different that there was no point in trying to bridge the gap. But that doesn't mean I haven't thought of her at all. The twins have been enrolled in ballet since they were three (Elaina loves it, Elizabeth has a little more trouble), and I know that Lily goes to the same academy as they do. I've seen her from time to time when I'm dropping off the twins or picking them up again. I guess I've kept closer tabs on her than I thought. But until today, we never really interacted. Not that me knocking her over really counts as an interactive experience.

I stop, breathing hard, and walk over to my desk to take a swig from my water bottle. The open screen of my laptop shows a new message—do I ever close this thing? Another rush of adrenaline floods my body. It's Diamondlily34, another private message. As the name comes onto my screen, puzzle pieces click together in my mind. Diamondlily34. Diamondlily. *Lily. Could it be her?*

Another image flashes into my mind: the pages I saw in Lily's arms. I was too distracted at the time to notice, but now it's all starting to make sense. I sit down and open Google, and the Miss Diamond comic opens onto my screen. Of course: *The Adventures of Miss Diamond* was a comic focused on a ballerina superhero, but it stopped running about eight years ago. The cover matches the stack of papers I saw in Lily's hands. I scroll down and find the author: Scott Kingston. Holy shit.

Diamondlily34 is Lily Kingston.

CHAPTER 5
lily

Modern dance is like a recess from ballet. I have it right afterward, and even though my muscles are already fatigued, it energizes me. The movements are so fluid and free that it's like a break for my mind. I lose myself in the beat of the music, in the ebb and flow of my body. I don't think about anything. I don't realize how much my legs are aching. I don't notice the sweat dripping down my forehead or the strands of hair stuck to my neck and face. The next thought in my head is the next move, and that's all. When the hour is up it feels as though it's only been a few minutes. I take a few extra minutes to cool down, stretching my hamstrings and my back. The bottoms of my feet are adjusting to the different strain of modern dance; I might not be putting the same kind of pressure on them as I am when I'm on pointe, but I think I'm getting a blister just from dancing barefoot. My feet are pretty disgusting, which I think is true for all ballerinas. My toes are gnarled and they still bleed sometimes after a class on pointe. Finally, I grab my stuff and head out the door.

"How was class?" asks my mom at the dinner table.

I know she means dance, not school. I'm expected to bring home A's, but other than that, my mom cares much more about dance. That's something we have in common, anyway—all I've ever wanted to do was dance. It's always been my plan to make a career out of it.

"Good," I say, in between bites of baked potato. "I had modern after ballet."

"Mhmm," says my mother.

"I got those boxes down from the attic."

She sets her fork down carefully on the edge of

her plate. My stepdad is working late, so it's just her and me on either end of the long table.

"I wondered when you'd go looking for those again," says my mom, surprising me. "Anything that was your dad's is yours, Lily, you know that."

And just like that, she goes back to eating. I'm surprised at her levelheadedness, but I let it go. When I'm finished I clear my plate and head upstairs two at a time. My room is my own haven, with a dark blue bedspread and white curtains, and books everywhere. I pull out my desk chair and sit down, opening my laptop.

I don't know what I'm doing, going on these stupid forums all the time. I might have read comics with my dad, but it was never an obsession. But it reminds me of him so much. He wrote Miss Diamond for me, because I loved superheroes and I loved ballet and I couldn't find a middle ground. He wrote a superhero just for me, one who wore tights and pointe shoes but also had superpowers and fought crime. I loved it so much. I have every single issue he wrote, obviously. He based her whole look on me. He would come to ballet and sit with a sketch pad, furiously drawing the tilt and spin of my feet, the contrast of my hair against the lights. When I wanted to wear a black leotard and tights, my dad was all for it. Black leotards were no issue—they were part of the dress code anyway, but black tights were not. And ballet dress codes are very strict, especially for elite academies like the ones I have attended. Miss Amelia wasn't happy about the black tights or that I wanted to dye my soft shoes black too. I fought it the same way when I moved to pointe, where the standard color was also pink. My mom strode in circles, arguing with my father and me.

"Why can't she just wear the same color as the other girls?"

"I like black," I said, and my mom turned her eyes on me.

"What kind of ballerina likes black more than pink?"

"Valentina," said my dad. "She's unique. She loves

ballet and she loves Batman. She's multidimensional. Why not go with it?"

My mom looked down at me, tucked under my dad's arm. She was an old-school ballerina, completely focused on fundamentals. If I was going to dance, I was going to do it her way. It was just another cliff separating us.

When my dad passed away, I put away the comics. It just wasn't the same to read *The Adventures of Miss Diamond* without him, or Daredevil or Superman or any of the rest of them. I've never talked about comics with Rob either, not that we talk about much that's important anymore. I just locked it all away, until recently when it started to spill out again.

My laptop chimes and I look up at the screen.

Sandman213 just logged on. This is who I've been talking to lately, even though I have no idea who he or she is. I've seen the user name in the chat room for the school club, so I assume it's someone from my high school, but I still don't know who. I don't really care. Whoever it is, I've had some of the best conversations since my dad died. It could even be a girl, but the fact that they don't know who I am and I don't know who they are is a kind of comfort. I don't have to put on an act or be the Lily Kingston that everyone thinks they know. I can just be who I am.

Sandman213: how was your day?

I grin. It's such a simple question, but one I guess I just don't get asked very often.

Diamondlily34: it was ok. How was yours?

Yeah, I know, kind of lame, but I'm new at this. Even though I've been chatting with this person a while, I still don't really know how much I'm supposed to share.

Sandman213: mine was ok too. Pretty quiet. Having trouble staying awake in class since someone has been keeping me up all night...

I smile again. That person would be me.

Diamondlily34: lol, sorry about that. I've been a little tired too.

That's an understatement. I almost fell asleep today between ballet and modern.

Sandman213: we could always meet in person, you

know. then we could hang out at regular times and not stay up until three in the morning :)

I sit back in my chair and consider it. I don't think this is the case in this particular situation, but I could be talking to someone totally creepy. I don't want to be that girl stupid enough to get abducted by someone she met online. There is another chime from my computer.

Sandman213: *we could meet somewhere public. Not trying to meet you in a dark alley or behind a shady bar or anything lol*

It's like they're reading my mind. I relax a little and cross my arms. A month ago, I could've never seen myself in this situation. I would've laughed if anyone had said I'd be visiting an online chat room everyday and talking to someone I'd never met in person. But with things going the way they are with Rob, I'm in a different position than I was then. I've been feeling braver, which seems like a para-dox, because I haven't been brave enough yet to tell Rob I don't think we should be together. I push the thought from my mind. That's a decision for another day.

Diamondlily34: *what did you have in mind?*

Sandman213: *there's a convention at the downtown center this weekend. It's the annual Seattle Comic & Graphic Art convention... sorta lame, but not a bad place to meet up, right? if you're down. It is a cosplay event, so a costume is kinda expected. But I don't think you have to wear one if you don't want to*

I know the event: it's held in downtown Seattle every year. Is that really something I want to get into, though? It's a hardcore comic book fan club thing . . . the nerdiest of the nerdy. I'd probably have to go in costume too, since cosplay is literally dressing up in your favorite character's outfit based on the event's theme. A part of me is thrilled at the thought—I would get to go somewhere where everyone loves comics as much as I do and talk about them all day. I can dress up as Miss Diamond or anyone else I want. It's tempting, but I'm not convinced. It's still far enough out of my comfort zone to make me think twice.

Diamondlily34: idk, maybe. Not totally sure I want to go to, but I'll think about it.

Sandman213: no pressure. But if you do decide to go, you should know I'll be dressed as Batman. There will probs be other ones there besides me, but that's my best costume lol. It's hard to go as Morpheus. I could, but he wears a kimono.

Well, that tells me I'm talking to a guy. I think a part of me had already gotten to that conclusion, because I'm not really surprised.

Diamondlily34: hahaha, too true. I'm sure you would look good in a kimono if you decided to rock it though. As for me, I guess we'll see. I'll let you know what I decide, and what I'm going as... or maybe it will be a surprise. :)

I shut my computer and grab my backpack, smiling to myself. It can't hurt to keep him on his toes. I pull out a notebook and open it to my history notes, but the words keep blurring in front of my eyes. I give up after a few minutes and decide to get in the shower, since I'm still sweaty from dance. My little bathroom fills up with steam and I inhale deeply before getting into the shower. I reach for the shampoo and take another deep breath—showers are my relaxation time. I need to let my mind go blank and just let the hot water pamper my aching muscles. Lately, I'm being pulled in so many different directions that I sometimes think I'll explode. I need to streamline what it is that I really want.

I turn the water off after ten minutes or so, briefly toweling off before pulling on my fluffy white robe. I rub a circle in the steam on my bathroom mirror until my face comes into clearer view. I see what I always see: a heart-shaped face curving into a decidedly stubborn chin, dark blue eyes, nearly indigo, strong brows. My mother's cheekbones and my father's mouth. It's a combination of other peoples' features molded into something unique. Sometimes, though, I have a hard time finding a shred of myself in my own skin.

CHAPTER 6
lily

"Is there construction going on over here or something?"

"Huh?" Rob's question jolts me out of the stupor I was in, staring out the window while he drives. It's Friday, and all I can think about is whether or not I'm going to the convention. We happen to be driving right past it on our way to one of Rob's friend's houses. I agreed to spend time with Rob weeks ago and couldn't think of anything to get out of it.

"I think they're just setting up for something," I say. "It's not construction."

"Oh, yeah, I see the sign now. It's that stupid

comic thing. You know, where a bunch of freaks dress up and hang out?"

"Yeah, Rob, I know what you're talking about."

I look out the window but he doesn't take the hint.

"Fucking weirdos. Have you seen the costumes? They dress up like Batman and Robin and all that. Like they are six years old."

"Yeah, I know." Please shut up.

"Stupid."

He drives past the convention center and I look at the setup with a pang of definite longing. I don't know where I fit in, all I know is it might be time to step out of my comfort zone. Maybe it's time to take a chance. Then Rob speeds up and the image of the convention center fades into a cloud of dust, like the picture in my head. I face forward, my elbow braced on the window and my chin in my hand, unsure all over again.

The small get-together at Todd's turns into a giant party and I'm stuck there since I came with Rob. It's nearing midnight and I'm almost asleep on my feet, but the sheer amount of noise is keeping me awake.

I sit on the couch, surrounded by people who I've been to a hundred parties with a hundred different times, and realize I don't really know anyone. I know their names and what kind of drink they like best. No one here knows my middle name or my birthday or my favorite color. And more than that, I don't think anyone *cares.*

"What's up with you?"

Rob sits down on the couch next to me, swigging a beer. He smells like sweat and alcohol.

"Nothing," I answer. "I'm just tired."

"You're such a buzzkill lately, Lily. What has been going on with you?"

His eyes are sharp and accusatory despite the alcohol.

"Nothing is going on. I'm just tired. I'm going to head home."

"Are you coming tomorrow?"

With a start, I remember he has a game tomorrow.

"I can't," I say impulsively. "My mom won't let me."

"When have you listened to anything your mom tried to tell you to do?" Rob snorts, shaking his head, but he lets it go. "I'll drive you home," he says, but I just laugh. As if I would let him drive me home drunk.

"No," I say. "I'll get a cab. But thanks."

He kisses me goodbye, snaking his hand under my shirt, and by the time I untangle myself from him my hair is a mess and all traces of my lip gloss have disappeared. The cab arrives and I duck outside without saying goodbye to anyone else. The night is cold and cloudy and a fine mist drizzles over me despite the fact that summer is nearly here. I step inside the cab and as we navigate the twists and turns to my house on the Hill, I find myself wondering how quickly I can put together a Miss Diamond costume.

CHAPTER 7
jacob

There's no way she's coming. I adjust the head-piece for my costume and greet another friend of mine who's just showed up at the convention. The Comic-kazes have a table where we're flyering anyone who might want to donate or join the club. Really though, we're just a group of kids dressed in costumes and hanging out at a place that is, to us, paradise. The convention center is packed with people, young and old and in-between, and everyone is in costume. I've seen about fifty Supermen already, but that's always one of the most popular. A girl saunters by in an Emma Frost costume and I do a double take. Emma Frost is characterized by her racy outfits—they're more like lingerie. Not that I think anyone here is complaining.

Some people wear the most elaborate costumes you could imagine—head to toe, makeup, everything. Girls do their hair like the character and spend hours painting their entire bodies green to look like Poison Ivy for a day. My Batman costume covers me from head to toe. It's my favorite one to wear because it's so simple. The bodysuit zips up the back and I pull on boots, the cape, and the cowl, and I'm set to go. I'm glad I'm in the air-conditioned convention center, though, because I wore this for the twins' fifth birthday and almost had heatstroke. A flash catches my eye and I turn around, my heart racing, thinking it's the jewel that Miss Diamond wears, but it was just a clutch of rhinestones on the Emma Frost outfit.

I don't know what I'm doing, thinking that Lily Kingston might actually show up here. She didn't show up yesterday. It's been almost impossible the last few days to act like I didn't know it's her in the chatroom. I told her about the convention hoping that she'd come and we could get that all out in the open so I wouldn't have to keep feeling like a stalker. I'm addicted to the way she talks to me online. She's still guarded, careful, but she's opening up. It makes me wonder whether she'll be that way in person or if she'll treat me like she did that day I ran into her—like I'm invisible. I go to shove my hands in my pockets and then remember my costume doesn't have any. Well, while I'm here I'm going to enjoy myself. Pushing the thought of Lily from my mind, I head toward one of the exhibits lining the inside of the convention center. The two-day event features games, film screenings, autograph areas, and a million other things happening that I'm not even aware of. I nudge past a pair of Spidermans (Spidermen?) arguing about the role Mary Jane plays in the comics, and then I stop dead in my tracks. Someone dressed head to toe in black, with a spot of light coming from the jewel on her head, walks into the convention center. It's Lily. She's here.

CHAPTER 8
jacob

I don't know what to do. My fingertips have turned to ice but I know my face is burning underneath my mask. She is dressed as Miss Diamond, the way I knew she'd be, and she pulls it off better than I could have imagined. She's wearing a sleek black leotard with long sleeves, black tights and ballet shoes, and the signature black eye mask. If I wasn't expecting her I don't know if I'd realize who was behind the costume. Her hair is slicked into a high bun, surrounded by a black velvet ribbon. The diamond glints on the crown of her head. Lily walks into the convention center and the way she moves makes it seem as though people should bow at her feet. Every turn of her head and arch of her neck is a dance waiting to be broken into. Her legs are long and slim and curved with muscle. She is looking for someone: she reaches onto her tiptoes in a seamless movement, and I'm impressed at her balance in the crowd of people until I remember that she does this all the time. I have to move. She's looking for me, I'm sure—I have to go and say hi. My legs are lodged in cement. I take a deep breath and force my feet to move. I've barely spoken to Lily on normal terms, ever. I knocked her to the ground once and now we're meeting dressed as fictional characters. It's so absurd I almost burst out laughing, and as I approach her, she's grinning, too.

"Hi," I say.

"Hi," says Lily, and a giggle escapes her mouth. Her lips are slicked bright red and all I can see of her eyes are the slits of sapphire blue in the mask. Her cheeks burn with the same color on her lips. Standing in front of her feels like a dream. The fact that she was brave enough to come here, to see me, is a dream.

"Your costume is awesome," I say, and it's the truth.

"Thanks," she says, smiling at me. She has a dimple in her left cheek that I can't stop staring at. "I wanted to wear black pointe shoes, but I knew there was no way I'd be able to walk around all day in those. Soft shoes were second best."

"Yeah, it's perfect. I'm really impressed."

"Well, look at you. That's the best Batman costume I've seen yet."

She studies me, tilting her head. "How did you know it was me? I didn't tell you what I'd be dressed as."

"Your handle," I answer. "I figured Diamondlily and Miss Diamond were related somehow."

"That was pretty smart," she says, still studying me. We're sandwiched in a corner, out of the sea of people rushing by us.

I shrug, avoiding her eyes. I don't know if she'll be upset to know that I've been aware of who she is for a while.

"And the lily in Diamondlily?" she asks in a quiet

voice, and I know she must know. "Did you figure out that part too?"

"I have my theories," I answer, and the side of her mouth quirks up. Her lashes are so long I can see them flicker outside of her mask when she blinks.

"I think you know," she said. "How long?"

"A few days."

"Were you surprised?"

"Yeah. I was floored."

"I still don't know who you are," she says.

"Me? I'm no one. You probably won't even recognize me, but we go to school together. Here."

I pull my headpiece off, bat ears and all, running a quick hand through my hair so it's not totally stuck to my head. I have no idea how I look after having been in a batsuit for three hours, but she gasps when she sees my face.

"Jacob," she says, and my name on her tongue does something to my pulse. "Oh my god."

"It can't be that surprising," I say, laughing as her cheek burn redder.

She laughs. "I guess not," she says slowly. I can

see the wheels turning in her mind as she mentally flips back through our conversations, searching for the details that make more sense now. "Still. You hid it pretty well."

"I felt sort of weird once I figured out who you were," I admit, and her face falls.

"Why? Because of . . . who I am?"

"No," I blurt out, still holding my headpiece. "Not at all. I felt weird knowing who you were without you knowing who I was. I didn't want you thinking I was, I don't know, some random stalker."

"You could have told me you knew who I was," she says.

"Then I wouldn't have gotten you here."

She laughs, tilting her head up to the ceiling. Her eyes are slanted upward, sparkling like a deep pool.

"Probably true," she says quietly. "I was so nervous. I almost didn't come."

"Were you that scared?"

"Yeah. I've never done something like this."

"But you dance onstage in front of hundreds of

people. And you're scared to come somewhere in costume?"

"Have you seen me dance?"

"Um." I look down sheepishly, but her lips are still curved in a smile.

"My sisters take ballet at the same studio that you do," I admit. "I guess I've seen you at a few of their recitals or when I'm picking them up from class."

"Right," says Lily. "Makes sense."

We stand there for a moment. I look her over and she looks me over, her long lashes shading her eyes. I wish we were alone, and just the thought of being alone with Lily makes my stomach clench.

"How long are you going to stay?" I ask.

"I don't know. Now that I'm here I might as well walk around and check everything out. No one can tell who I am, anyway."

So she's not totally comfortable with this side of herself yet.

"You definitely should," I say. "The exhibits are amazing. I have to get back to the Comic-kaze table."

"Oh, yeah. I knew you were involved with that club."

"I created it," I say, grinning. "But yeah."

"You really are a total nerd, aren't you?"

I laugh out loud, knowing she doesn't mean it offensively. We're both here in costume—it is pretty funny.

"Yeah, pretty much," I admit. "But it looks like maybe you are, too."

"Can't really argue with that in this outfit," she says. "Well, I'll let you get back. I'll talk to you later."

"Okay," I say, and just like that she disappears into the crowd. I try to track her dark hair in the rush of faces, but I lose her within seconds. My heart is still pounding so rapidly I press a hand to my chest, wondering if hers is doing the same. Lily Kingston. Who would've guessed it?

look over my shoulder so many times the rest of the day that I get a crick in my neck, trying to catch another glimpse of Lily. I see a couple other girls dressed as Miss Diamond, but neither of them have her grace or make my palms sweat the way Lily does. I have a good time until the very last minute, when I help pack up our table and head out of the convention center to be greeted by the oncoming night. One of my buddies helps me carry the table to my old Toyota 4Runner, weaving our way in and out of the crowd still trickling out of the building. I've changed into jeans and a sweatshirt, since I know from experience that carrying things in that suit doesn't work well. Then I'm sitting in my car, heading home, and alone for the first time today. Lily's voice is echoing in my mind, a musical track on repeat. I clench my hands on the wheel; it gives me a rush of adrenaline just to think about seeing her today. I've been on my feet since this morning, but I'm overly alert, energized. I tap my fingers on the steering wheel, her name running through my mind like a heartbeat.

The girls are already in bed when I get home, and my parents are watching a movie on the couch.

"Hey, bud," says my dad, as I walk in the door. "How was it?"

"It was great," I say honestly. "I had fun. Pretty tired, though. I think I'm just going to head to bed."

"Sounds good, Jake," says my mom, reaching for me. I lean down and kiss her cheek, then hug my dad. "See you in the morning."

I take the stairs to the basement two at a time, locking the door behind me. My room is quiet, peaceful, but right now it's making me restless. I turn on my TV to something stupid, trying to distract myself with the noise in the background. Maybe a workout will help take the edge off. I flip my computer open out of habit and plug in my earphones at the same time. I have a new message. I open it without thinking and then almost bobble my laptop off the desk in surprise.

Diamondlily34: I guess since we've met now, you might need my number so we can talk like normal people and not the comic freaks we are :) 864-555-7768

It takes me another two hours before I've calmed down enough to go to sleep.

I get up in the morning when the girls come into my room and start jumping on the bed, because there isn't really a choice to keep sleeping once a six-year-old starts poking you in the forehead.

"I'm coming, I'm coming," I mutter into my pillows, swatting Elaina away. I make banana pancakes, their favorite, and I stare at my phone. I feel like I should wait a reasonable amount of time before texting Lily. If a reasonable amount of time would happen in the next thirty seconds, that would be great, but I don't think she'd appreciate getting a text at seven in the morning on a Sunday. With a start, I think of Rob. Did he know she was there yesterday? Would he care that she's giving her number to another guy? If I were him, I'd be pissed. Maybe I'm not reading this the right way. Maybe she's looking for strictly friendship and I read the vibes from yesterday all wrong. My mom walks into the kitchen in her fuzzy bathrobe and slippers, squeezing my hand as a good morning. She serves herself a pancake and I go back downstairs to change for a run. I need some cold air and rain in my face to take my mind off of everything.

The day passes like any other Sunday—I go for a run, shower off, and watch a movie with the girls. My dad sits in his armchair and flips through *Great Outdoors: Northern Adventures*, his favorite magazine.

Every once in a while he stops and shows me a fishing pole or a tent he likes.

"I'm free in another few weeks to go fishing," he says. "Let's plan for three Sundays from now."

"Sounds good," I answer, sitting at the kitchen table. I'm doing homework methodically, even though I only have another week of school before summer break. I don't have much time before I have to get the twins ready and get them to dance class. Sundays were my day to be their chauffeur when they first started dancing, and it's a habit that's stuck even when my parents are free on that day now.

I glance at my phone over and over, wanting to text her but worrying about getting into something I don't want to deal with. Everyone knows she and Rob are together, and while I don't really care what his feelings are about the matter, I'm not sure that's a smart step to take. Chatting on a comic forum about (mostly) comics is one thing, but texting is something different altogether. What I should do and what I want to do are at odds. I tap my pen on the table, remembering the comic in Lily's arms, the way Rob twisted her wrist, the fury in her eyes. I remember the way she looked yesterday, dark and sleek as a shadow but radiating honest excitement, like a child. I unlock my phone and pull up her number.

To hell with the consequences.

CHAPTER 10
lily

The sun is still high in the sky by the time I walk out of dance, still breathing hard. Clouds shift above me, blocking out the brightest rays, and mist drizzles on my heated skin. I adjust my bag on my shoulder and root through it, looking for my phone. I'm still in my leotard, with sweatpants pulled over my tights. I unlock my phone and see a text from a number I don't recognize. Almost absently I open it and read it, until recognition slaps me in the face.

Hey :) How's your Sunday?

It's Jacob. It has to be. It came in a half hour ago, so I missed it because I was in dance. He does want to talk to me. My lips curve into a smile even as I tell myself to calm down and quit being a sappy moron. Since when do I get excited just because a guy texts me? There's a message from Rob too, but that just makes me anxious. I quickly type in a response; he'll be mad if I don't text him back.

With a start, I hear a chorus of voices coming up behind me on the sidewalk.

"I didn't *steal* your leotard, 'Laina," says a high-pitched voice. "I borrowed it."

"You're not supposed to without asking," says another miniature voice, softer than the first.

"Elaina is right," says a deep voice I instantly recognize. Oh god, oh god. There's nowhere to hide.

I turn around and there he is, walking toward the entrance of the studio with two golden-haired girls. I blink, but there are still two identical faces staring up at me. Twins.

"Lily?" His voice is deep, husky, but there's a tone of kindness that relaxes me. I look up and meet his eyes, which are already smiling. He's holding a hand of each little girl and that melts me a little.

"Hi," I say. "Uh, hi, girls. I was just finishing a class."

"We know who you are," says one of the girls, big blue eyes blinking at me in slow motion. "You're the best dancer at the studio."

"We watch you every time Jacob is late," says the other twin, bouncing on her toes. Their hair is done up in little golden buns, and for the life of me I still can't tell either of them apart.

"This one is Elizabeth," says Jacob, reading my mind. He tugs the girl on the left forward, who grins and twirls. "And this is Elaina." The little girl on the right hides behind his legs.

"It's nice to meet both of you," I say, leaning down. "I liked to dance when I was your age, too."

"When we grow up will we be as good as you?"

I'm touched. I remember watching the older girls dance at my old studio. They seemed like fairies to me, so light on their feet and so talented. It's strange to think that role has been reversed.

"You'll be even better," I say, and the one who

I think is Elaina grins at me, showing her missing front tooth.

"Girls, you're going to be late," says Jacob. "I'll be back to get you later."

They take off into the studio. Elizabeth stops and waves goodbye to me, and then it's just Jacob and me on the sidewalk. His dark eyes flash over me and my stomach flips the same way it did yesterday. So. It wasn't all a dream.

"I didn't know you had kids," I say drily, and he laughs out loud.

"Little sisters," he says. "They were my mom's, uh, fortieth birthday surprise."

"They're so cute."

"They're a pain in the ass."

I laugh. He is silhouetted by the sun's rays, his body outlined in shadow. He's tall, and from what I can see of his body in his sweatshirt, surprisingly muscular. His shoulders are broad, his legs long and lanky. His hair is a little messy, like he's overdue for a haircut. Almost as though he knows I'm staring, he ruffles it self-consciously.

"I'm an only child," I say. "So I can still appreciate little sisters."

"Help me babysit for a day and your mind will change," says Jacob, chuckling. It's sort of strange to see him in regular clothes, having a conversation with me like it's the most natural thing in the world.

"Do you have somewhere you need to be right now?"

Jacob's hands are in his front pockets, his shoulders hunched a little toward me. He scans my face and I bite my lip, telling myself to be rational. It's not a good idea. I have homework to do. My mom is expecting me. All true, all suddenly irrelevant.

"No," I answer, smiling at him. I shiver a little in the misty wind and he steps toward me.

"I get ice cream sometimes when the girls are at dance," says Jacob. "Just drive through Cloudburst and get myself a cone."

Cloudburst is the best ice cream parlor in Seattle in my opinion. It's only ten minutes away from the studio.

"That sounds nice," I say, and Jacob grins and

waves me forward and we head to the little parking lot in the back of the studio. Jacob aims for a silver 4Runner which I can see has two booster seats in the back. One of the back windows has a pink Barbie sticker stuck on it. I love the fact that he doesn't seem to care at all that he drives a car with booster seats and stickers. Rob drives a huge Ford truck, immaculately clean except for the mounds of dirty gym clothes in the back.

"Did you have a good time at the convention?" asks Jacob as he climbs in and starts the car. "I only saw you that one time."

"Yeah, I did. I didn't stay too much longer. I walked around for a little while and then left."

He nods, pulling out of the parking lot. I buckle in and try to calm my breathing. This is insane. I should not be doing this. But then Jacob turns and smiles a half-smile in my direction and every thought in my mind evaporates.

"So, Miss Diamond?" he asks. "Why's she your favorite?"

"She's a badass ballerina," I answer, laughing. "And she was written for me."

"She was?"

"Yeah. My dad was the head writer of that series. I wanted a superhero that could bridge the gap between ballet and comics."

"And your dad wrote that for you."

"Yeah. He was pretty awesome."

"Was?"

"Yeah. He passed away a while back."

"Oh, man." Jacob's voice is soft and low and makes me want to cuddle.

"It's okay," I say. "Really. It was a long time ago."

"I'm still sorry. For what it's worth."

"Thank you."

We drive in silence for a moment. There is a yearning inside myself that surprises me. Some part of me wants to tell Jacob everything, everything I could possibly say about myself. I've never wanted so badly for someone to understand me.

"Why is Morpheus your favorite?" I ask.

"A lot of reasons, I guess."

Jacob is driving with one hand, the other resting on the gearshift. Just looking at it makes me want to lace my fingers with his.

"He's complicated—dark and good and sinister all at the same time. And I've always had vivid dreams, so I liked the concept of a Dream King behind it all in some warped dimension."

"Makes sense."

"How did I never know you were into comics?"

"No one really knows. It was mostly mine and my dad's thing, and when he died it kind of got lost."

He nods as though he understands, and maybe he does.

"It's strange," says Jacob. "I feel like I know so much about you and nothing at all at the same time."

"What do you mean?"

"There's who you are when we're chatting online, and there's the you that I know from school. And now, there's the you who's sitting here next to me."

I can't breathe. This is such a strange conversation, but it's so *real*, and it feels like I'm finally breathing fresh air.

"I know," I say quietly. "I'm sorry."

"Don't be. I like all the parts of you I've seen so far."

My cheeks go scarlet and I glance at him through my lowered lashes.

"How were we total strangers a couple weeks ago?" I ask, and he laughs out loud.

"I know," he says, shaking his head. "This seems so crazy."

And it is. But it also seems right somehow.

Jacob stops the car and I realize we've made it to the ice cream parlor. I feel a little weird going in in my sweats and leotard, but I get out of the car anyway. Before I can say a word, Jacob comes over to my side of the car and tugs his sweatshirt over his head. What is it about a guy taking a sweatshirt off that's so sexy? He hands it to me and I shake my head.

"Really, that's not necessary," I say, but before I can get another word out Jacob tugs it over my head, so all I get is a mouthful of cotton. I reach my hands through the sleeves and hug myself. I catch the first real scent of him, husky and masculine with a hint of something fresh—pine needles? Jacob is just grinning at me, and then I'm grinning back at him, and we're just two fools who can't stop smiling at each other on the sidewalk in front of an ice cream parlor. Jacob realizes this first and breaks away to open the door to the ice cream parlor for me. I order mint-chocolate chip on a cone, my number one favorite, and Jacob gets rocky road. We traipse back to the car and climb inside and I rapidly lick one side of my cone so the ice cream doesn't drip onto my lap. I hear Jacob's slow inhale and I glance at him over my cone. His gaze is dark and intense and locked on my lips. My blood feels as though it's been replaced by volcanic lava. I bite my lower lip out of habit and his entire body stiffens, his hands flexing into fists. His eyes meet mine and I so badly want to crawl into his lap and lose myself in the feeling of his skin on mine. Someone walks by, talking loudly on their phone, and the spell is broken.

I turn forward again, buckling my seat belt, and Jacob puts the car in drive, but my body is vibrating like a live wire. His jaw muscles clench and it gives me delicious chills. I pull Jacob's hood over my head, tucking my face into the side so I can smell it.

"Thank you for your sweatshirt," I say.

"No problem," he says easily. "Although I didn't mind your leotard and sweatpants look."

"I just finished dance," I say indignantly. "I'm a dancer, not a model."

"I was being serious," says Jacob, even though he's laughing. "You looked perfect."

He looks out the window suddenly, as though he's embarrassed for saying it. I can't help myself; I reach for his free hand and lace my fingers through the spaces between his. He inhales sharply at my touch, and his fingers curve around to squeeze mine tightly. I am trying to remember to breathe and trying to absorb everything about this moment at the same time. His palm is broad, dwarfing mine. I skim my thumb over his knuckles and he shifts in his seat, his gaze still focused ahead. I watch the muscles in his jaw flex and it makes something deep within my body come alive.

"Am I taking you home?" he asks, his voice husky, and I snap back to reality long enough to answer him.

"Um, yeah. Yeah. I'm up on Queen Anne—take a left here."

He turns and as we continue toward my house I'm swamped with disappointment at having to leave so soon. But he's right—I need to go home. I need to go home and shake off this feeling that I will be leaving some vital part of me behind here, in this car with him. I inhale the tension, heavy and still, between us, but it isn't awkwardness. Rather, it's the things we're both leaving unsaid because once the words are released into the air there will be no turning back. Safer to keep quiet, to say goodbye and try and forget. But I worry it will be impossible.

I direct Jacob to my house and he pulls up to the curb and puts the car in park. Finally, he turns to face me. His eyes are a warm brown, like the bark of a redwood tree, and completely focused on my face. He reaches for me, releasing my hand, and traces my cheekbone with his thumb. I lean my head into his touch as though it's the most necessary thing in the world, and it feels like it is. His eyes stay on my face, and I wonder if he can tell how quickly my chest is rising and falling. He nudges the hood of his sweatshirt down, and I know I must look like a mess, with my hair still in my ballet bun, and the tendrils that have fallen down and stuck to my skin. He slides his hand around to the back of my neck, kneading briefly, and then traces my bottom lip with his thumb. I am electric, every nerve ending in my body brought to life by his touch. It's incredibly intimate, to have him caress my face this way, but I don't fight it. He pulls his hand away, sitting back in his seat, and I fight the urge to pull him back to me.

"I have to go get the girls soon," he says softly.

"Okay," I say, my voice raspy. I don't think my lungs are getting enough air. I unfasten my seat belt and grab the bag at my feet.

"Do you want me to text you?" says Jacob, and my head snaps up, a smile playing on the edges of my lips. His face mirrors what I imagine mine to look like, dreamy and amused at the same time. This situation is just so strange, but I'm starting to feel like I've known Jacob my whole life.

"Yeah," I say, nodding. "Yeah, I'd like that."

My phone beeps, and I look down to see Rob's name at the same time that Jacob does. Of course, this is the exact moment he'd choose to respond. It breaks the spell simmering between us, reminding me of the fact that, technically, I have a boyfriend. I meet Jacob's eyes hesitantly, waiting to see the sheen of judgment in his eyes, but there is none. He just smiles at me. I tug his sweatshirt back over my head and hand it to him.

"Thank you for the ride," I say. "And the ice cream."

"Anytime, Lily," he says, and I slam the door and run to my house before I can leap back inside and make an even bigger fool of myself. I open the door and slip inside without waving goodbye and lean against it, my head tilted back against the wood. What am I doing? I press my palm to my chest, waiting for my heart to slow back to normal. It thumps against my fingers relentlessly.

"Lily?" My mother's voice, cool and commanding. "Is that you?"

"Yeah," I say. I set my bag down in the mudroom and then pick it up again, knowing she'll make me move it if I leave it there. I run upstairs and throw it on my bed before coming back down again and heading toward the pantry. My mom is sitting on the couch with a book. Her hair, the color of corn silk, waves to her shoulders. Her shoulder blades are barely touching the front of the couch—it's been almost two decades, but she still has the perfect posture of a ballerina.

"There are bananas on the counter," she says as I pass her, heading into the kitchen. My mom is a banana fanatic—after a class she always insists I have one to refill my potassium level. I sigh and grab one just so she won't eye me disapprovingly from the other side of the room. I walk back out of the kitchen and stand on the hardwood floor behind the dining room, leaning on the back of the couch. My mom smells like fresh linen and her Elizabeth Arden perfume. I finish my banana and stand back up, stepping into a pirouette. I spin slowly, spotting the wall each time, over and over again. My body does the work for me, my muscles acting out of memory, and my mind drifts. I wonder if Jacob is thinking of me. I wonder if he's feeling like I am now, dreamy and a little dizzy, which I blame on him, and not the fact that I'm literally spinning in circles. *How did I know him for so long but never really notice him?*

"Keep your head up, Lily," says my mother. "Shoulders back."

I obey automatically before finishing with a sigh. I lean down to stretch my hamstring, wincing, and my mother turns and watches me.

"What's wrong?" she says.

"My hamstring. I think I pulled it doing *tour jetés.* I'm always off balance when I land."

My mother sets her book down on the coffee table and comes behind the couch to where I am still bent over, stretching the back of my leg.

"Do one for me," she orders. I move to the corner

of the dining room, push the table out of the way, and perform a *tour jeté*, wincing slightly.

"You need to use your back muscles," she says. "And keep your head up. That's it. The move should flow through you, with your muscles not against them. There you go."

She points her toe and raises her arms, and in a single stride across our huge dining room she executes a perfect *tour jeté*, finishing gracefully. My mouth falls open.

"Mom," I say. "You're so *good*."

"Where did you think you got it from?" she asks.

"Why don't you ever dance anymore?"

She sighs, fidgeting with the waist of her yoga pants. She still has the body she had at seventeen, tall and slim, light in the waist.

"You know I can't," she says. "Not with my back the way it is."

"You could teach."

Her head comes up and she studies me quietly, looking at her dark twin in the mirror. "That's not my life anymore."

"Do you think it could be mine?"

I've never asked her directly before if she thought I was good enough to dance professionally. I know I have talent, but I don't really know how much of it. I've seen old videos of my mother dancing twenty years ago, and she was breathtaking to watch. I could be technically precise in my movements and dance for the next lifetime and never have the quality she did, where she seemed to sparkle and catch your eye every time she moved.

"Yes," she says, and my heart catches in my throat. "Yes, you're good enough. But it won't be an easy life."

"I don't care."

"No, you don't. You have a fierceness of spirit that rivals even mine, I think."

I meet her eyes and she is smiling at me at last, almost regretful but without bitterness.

"You need to shower," she says, and the moment fades away. But she is still smiling.

"Yeah," I say. I walk toward the stairs.

"Come back down when you're done," she says. "If you want. I can put on a movie or something."

"Sure," I say, a little surprised. "I'll be back down in a few minutes."

I head upstairs, closing the door to my room, and start stripping off my sweaty clothes. I unwind my hair from its tight bun and let it fall down my back, shaking my head to loosen the strands. I grab my phone as an afterthought and see Rob's text again. I go still. It's time to cut that thread of my life loose—and it scares me a little. For some reason, I don't want to tell him. But I know that I need to.

My messages show another icon and I open it and see Jacob's number come up. I smile slowly, hugely.

The girls can't stop talking about you... you made quite the impression on them lol

I type a response.

they made quite the impression on me. btw, sorry if I spilled ice cream in your car :)

no problem. what are you up to?

About to jump in the shower. What about you?

I stop at that point, tossing my phone onto the

bed. I'll text him back when I'm done. This last week of school is going to be insane—thankfully, we're out on Thursday so that's only four days of Rob and Jacob having to be in the same building for eight hours a day. I hop into the shower and let the hot water wash over me, thinking of Jacob's smile, of his hand on my face, of his eyes on me.

CHAPTER 11
jacob

She's taking a shower. She's taking a shower right now.

While I know perfectly well she didn't tell me that in any sort of provocative way, it is still filling my mind with images that are, let's say, distracting. I can't stop picturing her perfect body, slippery and wet, with bubbles cascading over her skin. I remember the way her body looked when she was still in her leotard; her body is willow-slim, but etched with muscle. Her shoulders and arms were perfectly toned, rippling with muscle when she moved.

She's so perfect. She's like an image out of a fairy tale, Snow White come to life. When she grabbed my hand I thought I was going to explode. Her hands are slender and small, her wrists so delicate it looked like they were made of glass. I couldn't resist touching her face, just to see if the skin of her cheeks was as silky as it looked. Her face was flushed with color, her eyes wide and dark, nearly indigo. I've never seen anything so beautiful. She reminds me of a panther, lithe and graceful, but strong. Lethal. This girl will be my downfall, I can already see it. I can already see the ending. I can already see the free fall. Guys like me and girls like her . . . the fact is, I'm going to get cast aside at some point. I'm sure of it.

I already don't care.

I'm sitting in the living room with my family, a science fiction book on my lap that I'm not reading. I should keep working on my homework, too, but I'm too distracted. I can still smell her on my sweatshirt, a mix of cinnamon and vanilla. The way she looked at me after Rob's text came up was heartbreaking; it was like she was waiting for me to shut down, to judge her. But I won't. Do I wish she would break up with him—yes, obviously, just so I could be a little more forward with her without feeling like I'm infringing on the territory of another guy. But it's not my decision, and I won't tell her how to live her life when her and I aren't even—well, anything. Not yet.

I unlock my phone and type in an answer to her last message.

Just hanging with my family. Not thinking about you showering or anything.

Yeah, I went there. As soon as I send it I cringe a little—what a typical guy thing to say, right?—but there was so much tension between us in the car that my entire body is on edge. And I want to push her, just a little, in this direction so she'll sort of be forced into a decision in terms of Rob. Maybe it's selfish, but it's also a way to feel her out. How far does she want to take whatever is happening between us?

My phone buzzes and I nearly fling it across the room in panic.

Hahaha. Well if I ever need someone to wash my back, I'll give you a call :)

Holy shit.

I am definitely not getting any sleep tonight.

The next day of school is like a bad case of déjà vu. I'm just as exhausted as I was last week, except instead of chatting online with Lily all night, I was texting her all night. I'm tired and cranky and more than a little sexually frustrated. I'm a guy, shit—it doesn't take much. Especially with a girl like Lily.

I sigh, rubbing a hand over my face in my Anatomy class.

"Wake up, man," says Stephen, a friend of mine in the Comic-kazes. "All you do in class lately is sleep."

"I know, I know," I say, sitting up in my desk. "I'm here. I mean, I'm good."

Luckily, since it's the last week of school, there's not much going on anyway, especially for the seniors. Otherwise I think I'd fail out of high school at this point. I have to keep my final grades above C's to keep my college acceptance, but they're nowhere near that low.

I check my watch but there are still twenty-five minutes left of class. I unfold my legs from the tight space under the desk and head to the restroom, leaving my earphones in, just to keep myself from falling asleep.

The hallways are empty since class is still in session. I meander past rows of lockers and classroom doors, letting the air clear my head. It might nearly be summertime but today is cloudy and drizzly with a chill in the air. I don't mind it at all; there's nothing like the Pacific Northwest. The thought of being somewhere hot and humid makes me shudder. How do people breathe?

My pocket vibrates and I open a message from Lily as I turn the corner.

Can't focus. Falling asleep.

Me too. I went to take a walk to wake up lol

Where?

A rush of adrenaline floods my veins, snapping me to attention. Before I can text back a response,

I hear a door open. I look up and she's walking toward me, smiling. She's wearing blue jeans, faded white Converse shoes, and a gray hoodie. Her hips roll gracefully as she walks toward me.

The way she moves—it's like she's going to break out into a dance at any second. Even when she's just walking, I can see it. She moves silently, as light on her feet as a panther. As she gets closer, the gray of her sweatshirt makes her eyes look like rainclouds.

"Hey," I say, grinning, and she looks both ways, checking to make sure no one can see us, and then steps into my arms like it's the most natural thing in the world. She wraps her arms around my waist briefly, and my cheek brushes the top of her head. She fits in my arms like a puzzle piece that's been missing so long I forgot I'd lost it.

"Hey," she says, pulling away. "What's up?"

Hey, she says? As though she didn't just walk up to me in the middle of the hallway where Rob or anyone else could see us? Brave, for such a little thing.

"Just trying to make it through the day without getting written up for falling asleep in class," I answer, and she smiles, her dimple flashing. A classroom door opens and she jumps in surprise, and ducks, grabbing the front of my shirt and pulling me into the narrow area that connects the buildings. It's cramped and dusty and dim since the light bulb appears to be out.

"Do you think anyone saw us?" she asks. She still has a handful of my shirt, and her hands are pressed against my chest. I can't breathe. I can smell her hair, and as she shifts her breasts brush against me. After yesterday and last night, I am almost at my breaking point.

"No," I whisper, and she turns her face to mine. Our lips are inches apart, and there's enough room for her to back away, but she doesn't. Her eyes flick to my mouth and back to my eyes and I can't hold back anymore. In one quick movement, I duck my head and catch her lips with mine.

That first moment of contact is so powerful it surges through me like an electric shock. She gasps into my mouth and then melts, literally melts against me, and I'm in paradise. Too quickly, she pulls me under, so I barely notice when the rest of the world seems to go dark.

CHAPTER 12
lily

I can't get enough of the feeling of his hands on me. I shouldn't have even hugged him, not in the hallway like that. If Rob had happened by at that exact moment we'd both be dead. But I saw him walking toward me with that grin on his face and I couldn't stop myself. He is just so cute.

His hands slide over my butt and up my back and down again, stopping at my hips. He pulls me to him, almost roughly, and my body arches against his. I know I should break away, pull myself together, but my body won't listen to my mind. All I hear is his name in my head, the sound of his breath like a prayer coursing through my bloodstream.

I'm shaking with the tension between knowing we need to stop and the desire to keep going. But then he laces his fingers with mine and pulls my hands above my head and I lose the battle. It's so hard to fight against something that feels like light and air to me, something so completely vital.

Just one more second. Just one more kiss, and then I'll stop.

CHAPTER 13
jacob

We're pressed for time and in a public place where anyone could see us, but that just adds a layer of thrill. The fact that someone could come by at any moment heightens the experience and sharpens my senses, so that the feel of her lips against mine is multiplied.

She winds her arms around my neck and presses her body to mine. My palms are against the wall, on either side of her head. I don't trust myself to touch her; if I do, it will all be over. She bites my bottom lip and sucks it gently, and I groan. Her hands wrap around my shoulders, and she's clinging to me like a wet T-shirt stuck to my skin. Her lips are soft, and her hair hangs long and loose, shadowing us like a dark curtain.

I move lower, kissing the silky skin of her neck, where her pulse flutters. She is gasping, breathing hard, and I know my ragged breaths match hers. Her fingers dig into my skin, and I know we're running out of time but I can't bring myself to break away. She's so fucking sweet, and fiercely intense. She's a tornado, surrounding me in heat and the slickness of her mouth sliding over mine.

She slows the kiss down, moving her hands into my hair. Her tongue is a whisper over mine, slipping into my mouth and back again, teasing me. This is dangerous on so many levels. We have to stop. I can't stop.

She presses her mouth to mine again, branding me with heat and breath, and then breaks away, her chest heaving. I try to catch my breath, leaning down to touch my forehead to hers. She loops her fingers in the belt loops of my jeans and rests her thumbs on my hipbones. Everything this girl does is so damn sexy.

I hear the creak of a classroom door, and we both stiffen. The footsteps fade away and I relax again, but I know we need to move. I kiss her forehead, inhaling the scent of her, and she nuzzles the front of my shirt. Goddamn.

"We better get back to class," I whisper.

"Yeah."

She looks up at me and giggles, and I can't help but laugh, too, at the absurdity of the situation.

"I'll text you," I say, and she nods.

"Looking forward to it," she says quietly, and just like that she steps out of our little hallway nook and strides back to her class, innocent as a fawn. I wait for a few seconds and then walk out myself, turning in the opposite direction. I glance behind me at the exact same time she does, and both of us burst out laughing until I open the door to my class and she's gone from my sight.

I make it through the rest of the day, miraculously, and as soon as I get home I flop facedown onto my bed and pass out for a full hour. I'm not the kind of person who likes to nap during the day, so when I wake up again I'm totally disoriented. The front door slams shut and when I hear the voices of the twins and my mom I know that's what woke me up. I scramble up, pulling my shirt straight again, and go right back upstairs since I fell asleep in my clothes anyway. I walk into the living room and Elaina immediately attaches herself to my leg.

"I drew something," she says, handing me a picture of a butterfly, I think.

"That's great, 'Laina," I say.

Elizabeth is babbling to my mom about her day. My mom nods, following along. She moves to the stove and starts pulling out pots for dinner tonight. I follow, grabbing the strainer when she can't reach it. Elizabeth darts off to Elaina and my mom smiles at me, her eyes tired but happy. She has the same eyes as the twins, turquoise blue like jewels.

"How was school, Jake?" she asks.

"Good," I answer, with a yawn in the middle.

"Are you tired?"

"I just woke up."

"What?"

She blinks at me like I said I just got back from Mars.

"Uh, yeah. I was really tired."

"You never take naps," she says.

"It's not a big deal," I say. Moms get so concerned about everything. She knows me too well to think I'd just come home and go to sleep.

"Are you sick?"

"No, Mom. I was just a little tired."

"Were you on the Playstation all night? Your phone?"

As soon as she says phone, I know the flush is already creeping up my neck.

"Why were you on your phone all night?"

I open the fridge and try to act like I'm looking really hard for broccoli. Are all moms like this? Annoyingly nosy?

"Mom, I think we need to have a boundaries talk again."

"A boundaries talk about what?" says my dad,

walking in the side door. He scoops up Elizabeth and kisses her head, looking at my mom and me.

"Nothing," I say, but my mom interrupts me.

"Jacob took a nap today," says my mom, and I groan out loud.

"Jesus Christ. I'm eighteen. Can't I do anything in this house without someone poking their nose in?"

"Are you sick, son?" asks my dad.

"No, I'm not sick."

"He's been texting a lot," pipes up Elaina in the background, and I close my eyes.

"Oh," says my mom. "So it's a girl."

My dad looks up from the fridge, where he's grabbing a beer.

I sigh.

"You have a girlfriend and haven't even told us about her?" he says.

"She is not my girlfriend."

"So, it is a girl."

"Sort of."

I sit down at the kitchen table, rubbing a hand over my face. The kitchen table is old and cracked and has a stain on one end where Elizabeth spilled nail polish remover.

My mom sits down across from me, and my dad sits down next to her, throwing an arm over her shoulders.

"Well, tell us about her," says my mom, with a little too much enthusiasm.

"There's really nothing to tell," I say. "We're not even together."

"Why not?"

"It's complicated."

"Is she nice? Smart?" The question comes from my father.

"Yes. She's both."

"And you like her?" he says.

"Yeah," I admit, running a hand through my hair. "Yeah, she's cool."

My mom snorts. "She's cool. Please."

"Well, these things can be complicated," says my dad. "If you want my opinion, take your time. Let her know she's special. Spend time with her."

"I didn't ask," I point out, "but okay. Thanks."

"Listen to your father," says my mom, patting his thigh. "That's how he got me."

"Yeah, like my raw animal magnetism had nothing to do with it," he scoffs. My mom kisses him and pats his cheek before getting up from the table. My dad winks at me, then roars at my expression of disgust.

Soon enough, everyone heads to bed, and I'm the only one awake. I'm lying in bed and talking to Lily on the phone, keeping my voice low.

"Can you die from sleep deprivation?" she asks, and I laugh.

"Yeah, you totally can. But I don't think we're that bad yet."

"Yeah. Who needs sleep anyway?"

"Sleep is for the weak."

She giggles, making my stomach muscles tighten.

"I should go to bed soon, though," she admits. "I really don't want to."

"It's okay. You need sleep."

"I guess."

We both hover on the line, exhausted but unwilling to hang up. I listen to her sigh and I wish I were there.

"Are you in bed?" she asks.

"Yeah. I'm just laying here."

"Me too. I'm holding a pillow."

"Cool story, Lily."

"Shut up."

She laughs, and I smile in response. We're both punch drunk, so tired that everything is starting to seem funny.

"It's a miracle no one caught us today," says Lily. "We got lucky."

"I could've gotten luckier," I say, and she bursts out laughing.

"You're an ass."

"You like it."

"I do like you. I feel like all I want to do now is talk to you."

"That's how I feel, too."

There is a moment of quiet as we both consider the truth of those statements. I'm on the edge of a cliff and the ground is starting to fall away beneath my feet, and I don't care.

"I really should sleep," sighs Lily. "I'll text you in the morning."

"Okay, okay. Sounds good."

"Goodnight."

"Goodnight."

I wait for the click of the line, but it doesn't come.

"Do you need me to hang up first again?" I ask, smiling to myself.

"Yes," she admits on a sigh. "I can't."

"Okay. Sweet dreams, Lily."

"You too."

Her voice is soft and sweet, like melting honey.

I take the phone away from my ear and press End, falling back onto my pillow. My room is dark, lit only by the blinking of my charging computer. The quiet seems sudden now, obtrusive after the music of her voice. Now that I'm off the phone, I'm wide awake. I close my eyes and turn onto my back, trying to get comfortable. An image of her face swims into my head and no matter how hard I shut my eyes, I can't shake it. I see her midnight-black hair, her teeth biting into her full bottom lip. I flip over to my other side, but I still see her when I close my eyes. I sit up, running my hands over my face. This is hopeless. All of a sudden, my phone lights up. I reach over to where it's sitting on my nightstand and read a text from her.

Are you lying there awake, too?

I grin and start to type a response when I stop. I don't want to text her—I want to see her. It doesn't matter that I saw her eight hours ago. I want to hear her voice in person, see her smile. I can hear my heart beat in my ears in the dead silence as I sit there, considering. I get out of bed and tug on sweatpants and the same sweatshirt that I let her wear when we got ice cream. That afternoon seems like it was so long ago; so much is different now, but it's only been a few days. The rational knowledge that I should slow down, that she has a boyfriend, is all still there, but I'm already too far gone to care. I ease out the front door, shutting it an inch at a time, and sprint to my car.

It only takes me ten minutes to get to her house.

The streets are dark and deserted, spotted with streetlights. Lily's house is quiet, with curtains drawn, looming over the sidewalk. Everything is still and eerie, as though I'm in the middle of a dream.

I park across from her house and call Lily. She answers on the second ring.

"Hello?"

"Come outside."

"You're joking."

"Not me."

I hear sheets rustling and watch a light flick on in an upstairs window.

"Are you coming?" I ask.

"Yes," she says breathlessly. "One second. I'll be right down."

The line goes dead.

I sit and wait. Lily's house is so much bigger than mine. And with no siblings, there must be so much space. I wonder what it's like to come home and not have a six-year-old immediately clinging to you.

Sounds peaceful, but a little boring. I watch the front door swing open and a dark silhouette shuts it closed as carefully as I shut mine. I grin as I watch Lily come toward me. She walks at first while crossing the street, breaking into a run and then a sprint as she hurtles toward the car. I can't stop grinning, my heart thudding in my ears. Just seeing her makes my breath catch in my throat. She's wearing cotton shorts and a long-sleeved shirt that clings to her curves. She's the only girl I've ever known who actually looks perfect in pajamas.

Her footsteps pound in my ears and she rips open the passenger's door and launches herself into the car in one smooth motion, like a tiger pouncing. She doesn't stop but lands right in my lap, adjusting herself so she's straddling me in a tangle of hands and lips, and she sighs. Her mouth on mine is a fire, consuming me, until I'm reduced to nothing but embers in her wake. The restraint I had earlier today is gone, and my hands are all over her, sliding up her hips, where her shirt is riding up and showing inches of creamy skin. She tugs gently on my hair, grinding her body on mine, and I know my fingers will leave marks where they're digging into her skin. Her body is tight and toned, twisting beneath my hands. I slide the back of her shirt up to touch her bare skin, and she nibbles on my earlobe.

Just like earlier today, it gets too intense way too fast. I can't control myself around Lily—she saps all my willpower, drains me, and then fills me all over again with everything that she is. It's exhausting and exhilarating at the same time.

We stop again out of sheer desperation. Her breathing is rough and rapid, matching mine. I can't stop caressing her lower back, running my fingers up and down, barely touching her skin. She shivers, arching against me. I am hard beneath her, and I know she knows it. It makes it even harder to attempt to keep things relatively innocent. At this rate, they can't stay that way. We're both teetering on the cliff now, sashaying on the very edge. The only thing that's becoming more and more clear is that I'm not safe on either side.

"You smell like clean sheets," says Lily. "Clean sheets and . . . trees."

I snort, still running my fingers down her sides. She shudders and grabs my hands.

"That tickles," she says.

"You smell like cinnamon sugar," I say.

"That's my favorite body spray," she says.

We are quiet for a few seconds, her forehead tilted against mine. I wrap my arms around her waist and she presses her palm to my cheek.

The sky is dark outside the window, stars glittering like tiny diamonds, and in this moment I surrender to the fact that something is happening here that neither of us can control.

"How was dance?" I ask softly.

"It was great. I'm a little sore."

"Oh, yeah?"

I reach up and knead her shoulders and she makes a purring sound and arches like a cat.

"Yes," she says. "My shoulders are killing me."

"Dance is hard work."

"It is."

I keep rubbing her shoulders, working out the taut muscles. Lily leans forward and lays her head on my shoulder, draping her wrists around my neck.

"This is making me sleepy," she says.

"Good. Since both of us seem to be both exhausted and incapable of sleep."

"Yeah."

She sits up again, running a hand through her hair. It's like skeins of silk, shiny and so thick my hands get lost in it. I don't want her to go, but it's time.

"We better try to get some rest," I say. "For real this time."

She smiles and nods, sighing deeply. Her eyes shine silver in the glow flooding in from the street-lights.

"Thank you for coming to see me," she says. "I'm glad you showed up."

"Just wanted to say goodnight in person," I answer. "The phone wasn't cutting it for me."

We kiss goodnight over and over until finally

she disappears inside her house again. The silence is heavy, weighed down with the lingering echoes of our voices. I drive home in the quiet, letting my thoughts of her fill the empty space.

CHAPTER 14
lily

I have to tell Rob. I have to.

I can't keep avoiding him. It's Sunday now; graduation was yesterday. It was brief and tedious. It really didn't matter much to me since my plan is to join a company as soon as I can and start dancing. Not that I don't want to go to college someday—it's just lower on my radar. I wore the stupid cap and gown so my mom could take pictures and I walked across the stage and tried to act like I didn't notice Jacob at all, but I felt Rob's eyes following me. I wasn't surprised, not after how little I've seen him lately.

The final days of school were a whirlwind of Jacob. We haven't stopped talking once this entire week, except to eat and sleep, barely. I haven't really talked to Rob since last weekend, not for lack of trying on his part. I feel like he's been texting and calling nonstop, although it's totally possible that I feel that way because I've been so totally wrapped up in Jacob. I just shoved Rob to the side in my mind, which wasn't difficult because of how I've been feeling about him for a long time. Jacob wasn't the wedge that drove us apart; he was the catalyst that forced me to act.

We've been sneaking around all week, meeting at school in janitor's closets and the library. I've spent more hours kissing him in his car in the past week than the entire time I've spent kissing Rob since we've been together. The fear of getting caught or of someone else finding out is making me too anxious. I need to make a clean break with Rob. I know that. I've let things go way too far without being honest with him. Once Jacob and I started this whole thing I was so distracted that I put it on the back burner, but I think it's time now. It's not fair to either of them.

I still haven't decided if I'm going to tell Rob the whole truth. What's the point of telling him I've basically been seeing someone else behind his back if it saves him a little heartache to just say it's over? It would make me feel better to leave my conscience completely clean, but it seems selfish to me to make Rob deal with more pain just to ease my guilt. And there's not a lot of guilt, to be honest. What Jacob and I have been doing feels more right to me than Rob and I ever did. But I still have to tell him.

He's been bugging me to hang out all day, and I finally said I'd come over. Jacob understands, but that doesn't mean he's happy about it.

Just text me as soon as you're done, ok? I want to kno how it went.

I will. I'm going to his house now. I'll let you know when we're done talking

Ok. I'll be here.

I read Jacob's last text as I climb into my car, before I set my phone on the passenger's seat. I start the drive to Rob's, taking a deep breath as I go as fast as possible. Now that I've decided it's time, I want it to be over with already so I can stop any feelings of confliction. The anticipation is worse than the actual break up will be, I'm sure. Rob and I don't have much in common, and we've been drifting for a long time. I'm sure he knows that as well as I do.

I pull up to his house, parking and getting out of the car as fast as I can. I speed walk to the door and let myself in; his parents are used to me coming in and out. I glance around downstairs but don't see signs of anyone. His mom is usually crocheting scarves (I think) on the couch and his dad is either watching poker tournaments on the TV or shopping online on the laptop. I don't see either of them.

"Rob?" I call, and he comes hurtling downstairs.

"Hey, you're here," he says. He tries to kiss me and I turn my head away. When he's persistent, I let him peck me on the lips, but I don't respond. His face is twisted into a frown when he pulls away.

"Where are your parents?" I ask.

"They're at a golf tournament in San Louis Obispo," he says. "They'll be back tomorrow morning. I thought we could enjoy the, uh, place to ourselves."

"Uh huh," I say drily. *In your dreams.* Why I ever let this guy near me is becoming less and less clear to me.

"What's up with you?" Rob demands. He sits on the edge of the leather couch, leaning forward with his elbows on his knees.

"I need to talk to you," I say.

"About what? About how you dropped off the face of the earth this week?"

"Yeah, sort of."

"Well, do we have to talk now? There's a game coming on in ten minutes that I want to watch."

"You'll have to tape it, Rob."

"Damn," he mutters, rolling his eyes. "Alright, fine. That's fine. What do you want to talk about?"

I debate between trying to ease into the news and then decide to take the plunge. Rob seems to understand directness better, anyway.

"I don't think we should be together anymore," I say.

Rob's eyes narrow into pale slits. He lets the statement hang in the air, and I wish desperately that I weren't in this house alone with him. I brush the thought aside like a fly, straightening my shoulders. I'm no coward. And this isn't anything I can't handle.

"What are you trying to say?" says Rob suspiciously, and I nearly burst out laughing.

"Was that not clear enough for you?" I ask. "I think we should break up. I *want* to break up."

"Well, I don't."

I'm so floored that it takes me a second to recover.

"What do you mean, you don't?"

"I don't want to break up. I like being with you."

His jaw is set stubbornly, his arms folded.

"No, you don't," I say. "You don't like being with me. We fight and argue and we have nothing in common. Sometimes I think you don't know me at all."

"Sure I do."

"Oh, yeah? What's my favorite color?"

"Red."

"No. Red is the color you think I look best in."

"Whatever," says Rob, his face reddening. "It doesn't matter. That shit isn't even important."

"You don't want to be with me, not really. You want to be with the idea of me, maybe."

"I don't want you to be with anyone else."

I am dumbfounded.

"Rob, you can't try and be my boyfriend just so no one else can date me."

"You're mine," he says, gritting his teeth, and the words coming out of his mouth make my blood run cold.

"No, I'm not," I say, and I'm surprised at how strong my voice sounds. Inside I am starting to shake.

"Yeah, you are," says Rob. "And I'm not putting up with this bullshit. You don't think I don't know what's going on? You think I don't know you're already hooking up with some loser behind my back?"

"Rob—" I say, but he advances on me, stalking me like prey. I am suddenly hyperaware of the nearest exits, of how much bigger he is than me. I could never make it to the door before he caught me.

"I'm not stupid," he hisses. "And if you won't even fuck me, there's no way in hell I'm letting you go just so you can run off and fuck some other guy. You're with me. That's the way it goes."

I'm backing up in slow steps as he walks toward me, one step back for every step forward. I'm only a few feet from the door—if I could just distract him long enough, I could run. I don't care about this being a rational conversation anymore. I don't feel safe and I need to get away. Adrenaline pulses through my veins and through the paralyzing fear I find my voice.

"I'm not with anyone else," I say, raising my hands. "I just thought it would be good for both of us to get our heads on straight for awhile."

I'm talking nonsense, trying to calm him down, but it just seems to make him angrier.

"Why wouldn't you want me? You don't even know how fucking good you have it. Maybe it's time I reminded you."

He takes another step toward me and my resolve breaks. I whirl, groping desperately for the door handle, and my fingers just brush it before Rob's arms snake around my waist. I flail, shrieking, and he squeezes me like a boa constrictor until I gasp for breath. One of my legs connects to some part of him and he drops me altogether, so hard that I hit the floor with a resounding crash. I scramble toward the door, but he grabs my ankle and drags me back, hauling me to my feet with a grip so rough I know without a doubt there will be bruises. When I'm on my feet he shoves at me, his face a mask of rage, and in my fury I scratch for his eyes. He swats my hands away like they're mosquitoes, and in the scuffle he backhands me by accident right underneath my eye. My fear evaporates, replaced by a white-hot fury.

"I didn't mean to hit you," he says defensively, and I kick him in the groin as hard as I possibly can. He wheezes and bends at the waist before dropping to the floor and rolling into the fetal position. I aim to launch a kick into his stomach, and then drop my foot. I am not like him—I do not have a thirst in me to hurt anyone. That's the difference between me and him. I wouldn't hurt someone who couldn't defend themselves. I kneel down so I can make sure he hears every word I say. I am shaking from head to toe.

"You will never come near me again," I hiss, disgust in every word. "Never talk to me again, never call me, never come within fifty fucking yards of me, or I will call the police and have them lock up your pathetic ass. Is that clear?"

He glares at me, so I kick for his groin again. His face turns the color of dirty dishwater. He moans and mumbles and finally nods.

"Good," I say. "Goodbye, Rob."

I open the door and sprint to my car as fast as my feet can carry me, trying to shake off the sick feeling in my stomach from being trapped.

"Please, please," I whisper. I grab my phone from the passenger's seat and try to dial Jacob three times, but my hands are shaking so badly I keep dropping my phone. I know the tears are coming and shock is setting in. I have to call him before I fall apart right here. Finally, I press Call and hold the phone to my ear.

"Hello?"

"Jacob," I gasp, and then I am sobbing into the phone so hard I can't breathe. Jacob is panicking.

"Lily, talk to me. Are you okay? What happened?"

"Oh god, oh god, oh god . . . "

"Lily, where are you. I'll come and get you. Are you hurt?"

"No, I'm not hurt."

I gasp for breath, wiping the tears away furiously.

"I'm at 22 Alder Point Drive. I'm sitting in my car. Come, please."

"I'm on my way. Hold on, Lil."

The line goes dead and I curl my knees to my chest, my entire body wracked with sobs. I gasp for breath, trying to calm down, but the release of fear is too much for me to physically handle. I gingerly probe my cheek. I can already feel the swelling. I pull down my mirror and groan when I see my reflection. My cheekbone is swollen and red and already bruising. A shadow of purple is spreading across my face all the way up to my eye.

"Dammit, Rob, you asshole," I say. I close the mirror and cry, waiting for Jacob. I would have rather driven myself, just to get away from this house, but there's no way that's happening right now. I can't calm down long enough to catch my breath, let alone drive. A few more minutes pass with only the sound of my hysterical crying and finally lights pull up behind me. Jacob opens his door and gets out and I open my door, but when I try to stand my legs give out and I fall back into my seat again.

"Lily, what's going on?" says Jacob, and then he sees my face.

"You're fucking kidding me," he says. "He hit you?"

"He didn't mean to do this to me," I say. "But we were fighting."

"Is he still in the house?"

"Yeah."

I've never seen Jacob's face like this—it's set like

stone, and I can see the fury radiating under the surface like lava. He starts across the street.

"Jacob, no, please."

He stops a few feet off of the curb.

"Please don't," I whisper. "Please. Just come back. Don't leave me here alone."

At my plea he turns and scoops me up in his arms as easily as if I were a rag doll. He shuts my door with his hip and carries me to his car, setting me down in the passenger's seat. He helps me with my seatbelt as though I'm a child and then looks me right in the eyes. I am still crying, my shoulders shaking with the effort to hold back the tears. So lightly it might be a dream, he brushes the bruise on my face with his fingertips.

"I don't care if he meant to do this or not," he says quietly. "I hate that he put his hands on you."

He caresses my cheek gently with his palm and I cover his hand with mine, leaning into his touch. Just being this close to him calms me, steadies my heart.

"The girls are at a playdate and my parents are out," he says. "Do you want to come to my house?"

I nod. Not only can I not go home right now, but I don't want to be away from him. The thought panics me enough to start the tears flowing again.

"Just hang on, okay?" Jacob kisses my good cheek and gets back in the driver's side. He reaches over to hold my hand as we head to his house and his touch soothes me. To be touched by Jacob, with so much tenderness, puts into stark clarity how much my relationship with Rob was lacking. He skims his thumb over my hand and looks over at me every few seconds, just to make sure I'm okay. I'm calming down slowly but surely, breathing in the now-familiar scent of his car and letting it steady my nerves. I am safe here. I know that with absolute certainty.

We drive through downtown and into a suburb close to our high school. Jacob pulls into the driveway of a little brown house on the west side of the street. He puts the car in park behind a blue Suburban and then comes to my side to help me out of the car. I'm still shaky enough so that I take his hand when he offers. He wraps an arm around my waist and leads me down the driveway step by step. I hate the way my legs are trembling. I hate that I can't shake the sensation that I'm being hunted. I almost don't want to go inside Jacob's house because I'll be closed in again. At the thought, my eyes flood with tears all over again and I brush them away furiously. I refuse to let him have that kind of control over me. He isn't worth it.

Jacob opens the front door for me and I glance around as I step inside. He stands with his hands in his pockets as we walk into the living room and around to the kitchen and back. It's all an open design, and the house is tiny. There are pictures everywhere, of Jacob's little sisters in tutus and on their first day of preschool. I see, too, photos of a small, dark-haired child that I know must be Jacob. There he is, smiling a toothy grin in a plastic pool and holding one of the twins in the hospital. I can track his growth year by year—the evidence is every-where. I even laugh a little through the tears that are still flowing when I see a picture of him in a diaper with his head stuck in a cat door.

"It's good to see you smile," says Jacob quietly. He comes up behind me and rubs my arms with slow, reassuring strokes. I continue to explore, each step taking my mind farther and farther from Rob. The couch is worn and dark red and covered with the softest throw in the world. There are Barbie dolls and Legos and blocks everywhere—some in a pile in a basket in the corner, but more scattered on the floor. I catch a glimpse of comics, too—Calvin and Hobbes, Superman.

"I love the comics," I say, gesturing to the ones on the floor.

"There are about a thousand more in my room," says Jacob, laughing. He leads me down the stairs and into his room and shows me the boxes of comics. I gasp, in heaven, and Jacob laughs. His room is sparse, with the bed and a desk on the far wall. The TV and couch are on the other side, and a set of weights. It's messy and there are drawings everywhere, too, of characters I recognize, and some I don't. I sift through another box of comics, astounded at how many he has. Sometime, when I'm a little less shaky,

I want to sit and go through every single box. I take his hand and lead him back upstairs—the basement is making me a little claustrophobic right now. I want to be near the sunshine streaming through the upstairs windows and breathe until this feeling of being stalked leaves me.

"Sorry this place is a little messy," says Jacob, and I shake my head vehemently.

"It's great," I say, sniffling. "I love it."

And it's true. It's completely different than my house, which is spotless the majority of the time because my mom is obsessively neat and my step-dad works too much to make a mess at home. This house looks lived in. The floors might be scuffed and the couch has arms that are worn in, but there's so much life. The doorframe leading into the hallway is covered with black marks, and as I look closer I see the measurements of the past two decades. There are lines for Jacob at two, and the girls at four, and Jacob again.

"Elizabeth was always taller," says Jacob. "But Elaina caught up right when they turned three."

"You were lucky you got to watch them grow up," I say.

"I wasn't so sure when my mom told me I was going to be a big brother," he says, laughing. "I'd been an only child for twelve years. I thought life was pretty good as it was."

He shifts around so he's standing behind me, wrapping his arms around my shoulders as he continues talking.

"But something went wrong, right before my mom was supposed to deliver. One of the twins was in distress, and she had an emergency C-section. And I remember how afraid I was that she wouldn't make it. I sat in the waiting room and closed my eyes and prayed and prayed and when my mom came out of surgery and let me hold them it was the happiest moment of my life."

I look up at the picture on the wall, of a pre-teen Jacob with a golden-haired baby in the crook of each arm. He is staring down at them, his lips slightly parted, his eyes wide.

He turns me slowly to face him, inhaling sharply

at the sight of my face. He reaches up and traces the bruise with his thumb again, studying my face.

"Does it still hurt?" he asks.

"Not really. It's just throbbing now."

"I'll get you some ice. You can sit down anywhere you want."

He heads to the fridge and I move slowly to the couch, sitting down with a sigh. I lean my head back against the softness of the cushion and try to make myself relax. The adrenaline that flooded my veins earlier is ebbing away and leaving me weak and exhausted. I still feel like what happened wasn't totally real; it seems like a nightmare that I woke up from crying.

Jacob comes in from the kitchen with an ice pack wrapped in a dishcloth and lays it gently on my face. I wince as it presses against my battered face and sigh. I hope this bruise goes away fast; I don't want to have to see a reminder of what happened in the mirror for the next week. Jacob sits down next to me but keeps a few inches of space between us.

"Do you want to talk about what happened?" he asks, scanning my face.

"Not really."

"Can you at least tell me what happened?"

"I told him I didn't want to be with him anymore, and he got really angry. I tried to leave and he grabbed me. I kicked him and he dropped me but I couldn't make it to the door, and in the scuffle he hit my face. And then I kicked him in the balls."

"You what?"

"I kicked him in the balls."

Jacob's face is a mixture of amusement and shock.

"That's how you got away?"

"Yeah. I think he would've calmed down eventually, but my way was faster. And I was desperate to get out of there."

"I can't believe you did that."

"Why?"

I meet his eyes fiercely, challenging him.

"I guess I can believe it," says Jacob. "You are a force to be reckoned with, that much is clear."

He leans forward and kisses my forehead, threading his fingers with mine.

"I'm sorry you had to do that," he whispers. "I'm sorry any of this had to happen to you."

"It's okay," I say. "It's not okay that it happened, but I'm okay now. Rob is never going to come near me again."

"I wouldn't think so," says Jacob. "And he better not."

I kiss his knuckles, one after the other.

"Thank you for not going in after him," I say. "I couldn't have dealt with any more violence or drama."

"I wanted to kill him."

"I know."

"I still do."

A smile curves at the edges of my lips.

"I'm okay," I say. "Really. You're doing a lot more for me by taking care of me than beating him up."

"I guess you're right."

He grins at me and, as always, I can't help but smile back.

"Do you want to watch a movie or something?" he asks. "Something low key?"

"That sounds perfect," I say.

"Your choice," he says. He grabs a box from the side of the couch and starts flipping through it. There is a multitude of Disney movies and old video games, '80s movies, and some really manly live action ones.

"I don't really care," I say.

"You can be honest," says Jacob. "We'll watch whatever you want."

I grab *Cinderella* from the pile and hand it to him.

"Sounds good," says Jacob, sliding the DVD into the player. "One of the girls' favorites, too."

"She's my favorite princess," I say. "One of them, at least."

"You like Disney princesses and badass comic book characters?"

"Why can't I like both?" I say indignantly. "I have more than one interest."

"I know you do," says Jacob. "You're impossible to pin down."

"Is that a bad thing?"

"No, not at all. I just can't predict you."

I nod. I know what he means. It's not something I can change about myself. Jacob is still sitting a few inches away. I scoot closer on the couch, tucking my legs up beneath me, and nudge my head onto his shoulder. He kisses my head but doesn't touch me otherwise, and I look up at him, frowning.

"Do you not want me so close to you?" I ask.

"No, God, no. I'm trying to give you your space."

"Why?"

"I don't know. I thought you might want some after what happened today."

I shake my head, hair falling into my eyes.

"You didn't hurt me," I say. "He did. You make me feel safe."

"Do I?"

"Yeah. That's why I called you, and no one else."

"Come here," he says quietly, and I swear my blood ignites. I lean forward, letting the ice slide from my cheek. Jacob turns toward me and I crawl into his lap. He slides a hand into my hair and his lips brush over mine, slow and soft, drawing the moment out, lengthening the seconds. I sigh, and finally relax, letting him draw me down into the place I'm getting addicted to, where it's just us and nothing else. Despite all I've been through today, no part of me shies away from Jacob. I reach down and touch his forearm, caressing the inside of his wrist with my thumb. He leans back and brushes the hair out of my eyes with his other hand, his fingertips branding me with a touch that might break my heart with tenderness. He looks at me like I'm something precious, a candle flame in the heart of the world, drawing him into the light. We sit like two statues, his hand on my face, neither of us willing to move. His eyes are dark and rich, and so intense it stops my breath. He shifts on the couch so he is sitting with his legs extended, and pulls me into his embrace, my back to his front. I lay my head back on his chest and my eyes flutter shut as he smoothes my hair back from my forehead. When he threads his fingers through my hair I groan.

"Did I pull your hair?"

"No," I sigh. "This is just the best feeling in the world."

He leans forward, kissing my temple, and *Cinderella* starts playing. I let myself drift on a cloud of exhaustion and peace. Jacob's hands in my hair calm me and the familiar music in the background makes me feel at home. I float, dozing like a cat in the sun. After a few minutes I turn my head and snuggle closer to him, so my nose is nearly pressed against his neck. He wraps his arms around me and I fall asleep to the sound of his heartbeat, steady in my ears.

CHAPTER 15
lily

I'm in the middle of a baseball field, surrounded by people who are screaming at me to run the bases, and I have no idea why. The sky is dark and purple and thunder rumbles. I start running, confused and disoriented, and the voices get louder and louder.

I wake up to four pairs of eyes staring at me still lying on the couch. I blink like an owl, at a total loss.

"Hi, guys," says Jacob, and I leap to my feet, smoothing my shirt down and hoping to God my hair looks somewhat respectable. Jacob stands too. His sisters are standing in front of us, flanked by who I think are his mom and dad. His dad is huge and burly, his mom petite. She has Jacob's dark hair. There is a long, drawn-out moment of quiet. I thank God that Jacob and I are, at the very least, fully clothed. I take a deep breath and decide I might as well take the first step.

"Hello, again, girls," I say, smiling at Elizabeth and Elaina.

"Hi, Lily," says Elizabeth. "Why are you on our couch?"

"I was watching *Cinderella*," I say, and Jacob's father grins. Elaina squeals.

"That's our favorite!" she says. The two meander over to the DVD box, arguing over what they want to see next, and we're left with Jacob's parents.

"Guys, this is Lily," says Jacob. "Lily, this is my mom, Sandra, and my dad, Greg."

"It's great to meet you," I say, stepping forward to shake each of their hands. They still seem a little surprised to see me, and I don't blame them, but at least they don't look mad. They're both smiling now, actually, their eyes flicking from me to Jacob and back again.

"It's really nice to meet you, Lily," says Sandra. "Are you staying for dinner?"

"Um."

I turn to glance at Jacob, who shrugs.

"You're more than welcome," says Greg. "We'll make another place at the table. Come on, honey." He tugs his wife's arm and the two disappear into the kitchen. I spin slowly to look at Jacob, who is fighting a smile.

"Well, that's one way to introduce you to my parents," he says. "Do you mind staying?"

"Not at all, as long as it's fine with you."

"Of course."

"Does my face look awful?"

He skims over my bruise with his thumb, then shakes his head.

"It's not as bad. It's still sort of purple but not as swollen."

I guess I'll have to live with that. Jacob takes my

hand and leads me into the kitchen, and I link my fingers with his. This day has been such a whirlwind, but nothing centers me more than Jacob's hand in mine.

She astounds me.

She fits in with my family seamlessly. She sits next to Elaina and gives her dessert to Elizabeth, who climbs onto her lap to finish it. She eats spaghetti and meatballs and laughs when Elizabeth gets marinara sauce on her nose. She makes my dad laugh and she offers to help clear the table when we finish, waving away our protests. I wish she would stay still; that bruise still shimmers in the light every time she turns her head, but she is a bundle of energy. I don't know how she manages to go from zero to sixty so quickly. She was sobbing in my arms earlier today and now she's laughing with my mom about something that happened on *So You Think You Can Dance?* the other night. I can't keep up with her, but I'm learning not to try. Just to catch the edge of her energy is enough for me. Finally, I tell everyone I need to take her home.

"Come back soon, Lily," says my mom, giving her a hug. "It was a pleasure."

"I will," she promises. "Thank you again for having me."

"No problem," says my dad. "We'll see you soon."

I manage to detach Elaina from Lily's leg and we make it out the front door. The quiet seems sudden, and Lily shivers in the night air, smiling at me.

"I'm sorry about them," I start, but she stops me.

"Are you kidding? I had a great time."

"I know they can be a little much."

"No way."

I open Lily's door and she climbs inside while I move around to the driver's side.

"I love my family," she continues as we drive away. "My mom, and even my stepdad. They're the only family I have. But I've never had something like you have—noise and chaos and messes. I liked it."

Her voice is quiet, wistful. I realize that Lily is lonely in her house on the Hill sometimes. I reach over and squeeze her hand and she smiles at me. God, every time I see that bruise on her face I want to drive back to Rob's house and kill him. I thought I would, too, when I first saw her. I've never seen anyone so panicked. All I could think of was calming her down again, of keeping her close.

"I guess I'm officially single now," says Lily. "It didn't really go the way I planned, but at least I'm not dating him anymore."

"I'm glad of that, too," I answer.

"Have you had girlfriends before? I can't remember seeing you with anyone, but I could be wrong. I hope that question doesn't embarrass you."

"Uh, no, not really. I dated that girl, Hillary, for a while? Really briefly. And that's about it. Mostly just me and my nerdy comics, my family, and working out."

She nods, and the question that comes to the

forefront of my mind is whether or not she and Rob were intimate. The thought makes me sick, but it could be true—they dated for a while.

"Were you and Rob close?" I ask. "During the good times, I mean."

"Not really," sighs Lily. "I never felt very close to him."

"What about physically?"

There. I said it. The question hangs in the air like fog, sticking to our skin. Lily turns and I can feel her eyes on me even as I focus on the road.

"No," she says, and a weight frees itself from my chest. "No, never."

"I was just wondering," I say.

"No. It never happened."

I breathe a quiet sigh of relief. Lily is feeling more and more like *mine*, and the last thing I want to picture is another guy touching her body. I deliberately change the subject to get my mind off of her body under mine, or, unpleasantly, under his.

"Do you want me to take you to your car, by the way?"

She sighs.

"Yeah, you'd better, so I can drive it home. I forgot about that."

"It's no problem."

I head to where I picked her up earlier, holding her hand in the silence. Lily is quiet, pensive, and I let her have her space. She's had the kind of day that no one should ever have to go through. I pull up behind her car and stop. Lily's eyes are pools of still water in the light of the moon, her hair a shadow. I pull her toward me and kiss her softly, inhaling her scent that seems to arrow straight through my skin. It's building again, that tension between us, so thick it's hard for me to breathe. I want to pull her onto my lap and touch her bare skin, teach her she can trust me, but I'm worried that isn't what she needs right now.

"I'll text you," I say. "Okay? And let me know if you need anything."

She is still, watching me. I look away so I don't drown in those eyes. I might never come out again.

"Okay," she says. "Thank you for today, for everything."

"Of course."

She climbs out and gets into her car. I watch her start the engine and drive away before I put the car back in drive and head home, already missing her. My body is on edge, wired, and I rub a hand over my face. She was serious on the way home; it wasn't the time to try anything. But, God, I wanted to. I feel so much for her that it's literally too intense for my body to handle. I had to get her out of the car just so I could drive away and not take her hand again and never let go. I get all the way home and into the driveway before I lay my head down on the steering wheel. I am already craving her. There's something in her eyes, or the way she moves, that completely entrances me. After today, there's a protectiveness for her that's growing inside me, too. How am I going to sleep tonight? How am I supposed to turn off this need for her that's clawing at the inside of my chest?

My phone buzzes. I look down, feeling that

physical jolt that comes from just seeing her name. She's calling me.

"Hello?"

"Come back." Her voice is pleading, intense. Every muscle in my body stills, tenses.

"Now?"

"Yes. Please. Please, Jacob . . . "

"I'm coming. Hold on."

I hang up and start the car again. My hands are shaking and my mouth is dry as I speed to Lily's house as fast as I can. I pull up to the curb and get out of the car, reaching for my phone.

"I'm here," I say into the phone.

"Come inside. They're not here; my mom left a note. They're staying the night in Portland because of some conference Paul had to go to."

"Okay," I say, striding across the street. "I'm coming." I can't stop grinning. My entire body is trembling. I've never been so exhilarated and so terrified at the same time. I reach her door and she opens it before I can knock.

She is wearing a black tank top and the pajama

shorts I'm starting to recognize. Her hair is a black cascade raining over her shoulders, her cheeks flushed.

"What took you so long?" she says, and then she is in my arms.

Everything but her mouth on mine is lost, disappearing into oblivion as I stumble into Lily's house with her legs wrapped around my hips. She tangles her hands in my hair and her mouth is slick and hot over mine. We kiss hungrily, furiously, as though I've been gone for years rather than twenty minutes. All of the day's frustration explodes out of me—her touch has destroyed my self-control. I bite her bottom lip before running my tongue over it, hearing the moan escape her lips. I can't stop running my hands over her back, down the backs of her legs where the muscles are bunched tight and strong. I slip my palms under the back of her shirt and she whimpers against my lips, biting my lip restlessly as I touch her bare skin. We bump into something with a thud, and I realize it's a wall.

"Sorry," I say into her lips.

"Don't be," she whispers. She unlocks her legs

from my waist and slides down my body, slowly, every inch of her brushing against me. I glance around at the huge foyer, the leather couch, until Lily pulls me upstairs. Her shirt is scrunched up, showing a few inches of skin that distract me enough that I nearly trip over the last stair. The upstairs hallway is hardwood, dark and shiny. Lily leads me straight, opening the door at the end.

"I thought you'd want to rest," I say.

"You thought wrong," says Lily. "I only want you."

Her words ignite my blood. I catch a glimpse of white sheets and a blue comforter, a full-length mirror, and a white desk before Lily shuts off the lights. The moonlight streams through the huge window beside her bed, making Lily look like she's glowing.

"I missed you as soon as you left," she whispers, taking a step toward me.

"Me, too."

"Why didn't you tell me to stay with you?"

"I wanted to give you space if you needed it."

Lily reaches for the bottom of her tank top, her eyes on mine. She pulls it off an inch at a time, unveiling herself to me. Her waist is tiny, her hips a subtle curve. Her skin is creamy and flawless, and when she lets her shirt fall to the floor, I'm motionless. Her breasts are firm and full, tipped with ruby. The moonlight plays with her hair, shimmering against the silky strands. She is too beautiful for me to know how to process it. I want her so badly that every part of my body is aching. She steps toward me, reaching to pull my shirt up and over my head in one sweep. Tracing my hips with her thumbs, she takes another step closer to me and I tumble us both onto the bed.

With Lily on her back, I shift so I'm lying on top of her, in between her legs. I lift myself up on my elbows to kiss her neck, starting at the soft spot under her jaw and working my way down. She writhes under me as I move down her body, gripping handfuls of sheets in her hands. She gasps when I slide my tongue over the underside of her breast, my hands moving to span her ribcage. She is delicate but strong at the same time, intense and easygoing, feisty, and heart-achingly sweet. She's everything, all wrapped up into one incredible, confusing, frustrating, perfect package.

I tangle one of my hands in her hair, the other flowing down her waist as my mouth finds her breast. Lily arches off the bed, pulling my hair, her voice a soft moan. I skim over the back of her leg, and her hips writhe beneath me. I caress her with my tongue, unable to stop myself lavishing attention on her body. I could do this all night, this slowly, until we both lost our minds.

Lily gasps as I graze my teeth over her nipple, and then she flips us over so she's straddling me, my back pressed into the mattress. The sheets are somewhere at our feet in a wild tangle as she kisses me over and over again and even as I try to remind myself to slow down I can't seem to stop my hands from roaming over her naked back and around to cup her perfect breasts. She grinds her hips over mine, and my jeans and her pajamas are frustrating barriers. I'm surrounded by the scent of cinnamon sugar and the dark curtain her hair throws over us. Lily's lips move to my chest, little sucking kisses that make me grit my teeth with pleasure. She bites lightly at my jawline and I groan as she shifts her hips over mine, teasing me. I'm hard as a rock, and I know she knows it. But I see no hesitation from Lily, no second guessing. I reach for the drawstring of her shorts and look into her eyes. She nods, lifting her hips so we can shimmy them off of her and onto the floor. She unbuttons my jeans, both of us rolling in a heap to our sides so she can work them off my hips and onto the floor, where they disappear just like the rest of our clothes. There is nothing between us any longer.

Lily stills, lying on her side in my arms. She slides a silky thigh in between mine, and I reach behind her to caress her backside. Her body defies description. She is all lithe muscle and soft curves, the perfect combination of soft and strong. Her skin is so silky I'm afraid it's going to disappear in my mouth like whipped cream. Her chest is rising and falling rapidly, her breath rushing over me. I kiss her cheeks, her forehead, her chin, and skim my hand over her hip. Her eyes are focused on me, the nails of her hand digging into my back as I reach between her legs. She is hot and wet, her body beckoning to me. She buries her face in my neck, shuddering as I stroke her gently.

"Please," she gasps, "please," and I move above her so Lily is lying on her back, her hair a dark fan behind her. I kiss her breasts desperately, her neck and finally her mouth, and she shudders beneath me.

"I trust you," she says.

I get up and search for my jeans on the dark floor, yanking a condom out of my pocket. Thankfully, the school nurse has them in a huge box in her office and I snag some every time I go by—just in case.

I walk back over to the bed and rip open the package, trying to fit it over myself. The condom slips out of my hands in my haste. Lily sits up, pushing my hands away.

"Let me," she says. She slides it over me, achingly

slow, fumbling a few times. Her touch is butterfly-light, and still makes me grit my teeth.

"Are you okay?" she asks, concerned.

"Yeah," I gasp. "I'm fine. You're fucking perfect."

I fall on top of her, cradled in the lee of her legs. She reaches up, running her nails lightly down my back as I kiss her, trying to pour everything I've been feeling into that connection.

"I don't want to hurt you," I say.

"It'll be okay, Jacob."

Her plea darts straight to my heart. I lean over her, positioning myself between her legs as best I can. She reaches down and guides me and I move as slowly as possible. Her body surrounds mine and I don't know if I can survive the pleasure. She winces as I move deeper, and I stop, trying to keep the weight of my body up and off of her to avoid hurting her.

"Are you okay?" I ask, leaning down on my elbows.

"Yeah," she says, but I can hear the pain in her voice. I stop halfway inside her, my muscles uncomfortably clenched, trying not to move. We're in a tangle of legs and arms. A flush rises onto my cheeks for the first time as the moment lengthens. I feel awkward and inept as we both remain motionless. Her eyes are pinched shut, her teeth clenched. Stopping now isn't exactly easy for me, but I draw myself out of her slowly and we fall apart, both gasping for breath. She flings an arm up over her forehead, lying on her back.

"I'm sorry," I say.

"It's okay, Jacob. Just give me a minute—I wasn't expecting . . . "

"I know. It's alright."

She shifts toward me in the dark, laying her head on my chest. I stroke her back. I don't mind stopping at all to avoid hurting her, but my body is a jumble of nerves. Every time she shifts against me even the slightest bit, I'm jolted with a pleasure so keen it borders on pain.

"Are you okay?" she asks, bracing herself up on my chest.

"Yeah," I say, trying not to grit my teeth at her touch.

"Why are you so tense?"

"Um," I stammer, and her smile flashes in the dark. "This is my first time."

"Mine too." She says, "It's gonna be okay. I love the way you care about me. When I'm with you I feel alive."

"Me, too," I whisper, as she starts to kiss my neck. "Lily . . ."

She pulls me toward her and I roll, flipping us so I'm on top of her again. Desire returns in a flood, stronger than before, and her touch removes all traces of awkwardness. Before I know what's happening, I'm leaning over her again, and she's guiding me closer, whispering in my ear.

"I don't want to hurt you," I say.

"I know. It's okay, Jacob . . ."

Her voice is low and breathy and she's encouraging me with her words and her body rocking against mine but I'm still trying to be gentle.

I ease forward, trying to be easy, but it's harder to hold back. I move another inch forward and she surrounds me completely with a little gasp and it's so fucking incredible I think I'll lose my mind. I start to move, watching her face closely. She reaches up to kiss my throat, moaning against my skin, and I move faster.

"Oh," she whispers, her shoulder blades bowing off the mattress. "Jacob."

My name is a whisper on her tongue, but it's everything. This moment is more than I ever knew was possible, more than I ever expected. I wind my hands in her hair and bury my face in her neck, completely undone. She wraps her legs around my waist and her arms around my shoulders, clinging to me as though she can't get enough either, like this moment might actually be real. She moves her hips in tandem with mine, and I've never felt so close to someone. Our bodies are connected, her breasts pressed to my chest and our hands pulling each other closer and our minds are the same way. I speed up and Lily matches me, her hips rising and falling like her breaths. Everything builds and builds until I know I'm on the edge of the world waiting to fall. Lily moans in my ear and gasps and we disappear together, leaving everything behind except the moonlight on her skin and the somehow certain knowledge that nothing will ever be the same.

Afterward, he cradles me on his chest, his fingers running through my hair. We lie there for so long, drifting with each other between awake and asleep. Finally, I sigh, throwing a blanket over both of us. I'm completely spent, physically and emotionally. Jacob's arms surround me under the blanket, holding me close.

I dream, I think, a dream where I'm dancing on a white stage while clouds swirl around my pointe shoes like cotton candy. From my shoulder blades, white wings unfurl, glittering in the sun. I spin faster and faster, perfectly balanced, closer and closer to the sun, my face tilted toward the light.

Jacob's touch wakes me, drawing me back to earth. I reach for him in turn before I'm even fully awake, still tangled in the last fading wisps of the dream. His hands skim over my ribcage, firm and gentle all at once. I find his lips with mine, sighing, my body heavy and lazy with desire. We shift, roll among the blankets, and Jacob finds another condom and both of us still fumble a little trying to put it on, me hindering more than I'm helping. He grips my hips and I wince a little at the pressure, but the pain is gone before it can really register. He moves, and my body moves to meet his, like a dance to music that only we can hear.

CHAPTER 18
jacob

The sun streaming in through the window wakes me, and for a moment I don't know where I am. I turn and see Lily on the sheets next to me, and everything comes flooding back. She is still sleeping, an arm folded over her breasts and her other hand tangled in her own hair. I sit up, rubbing a hand over my face. I'm not sure that last night was real; it seems much more likely that I dreamed it all, that I'll wake up in a second in my own bed.

Shit. My own bed. We fell asleep. I'm still at Lily's.

I leap up, tossing sheets and pillows aside on the floor, searching for my clothes. What time is it?

"Jacob?" Lily's voice is sleepy and sexy. She sits up and rubs her eyes and then reaches up to stretch, totally comfortable in her own skin.

"Good morning, Lily," I say, kissing her briefly before I return to my search. I find my shirt in a pile under the sheets and tug it on.

"Is everything okay?" she asks.

"Yeah," I say. "I just have to get home. My parents don't know I'm gone."

"Oh, shit."

"Exactly."

"What time is it?"

Lily leans over to her nightstand to check her phone.

"It's only six," she says. "Will your parents be up yet?"

"Not if I hurry," I say. "Sorry I can't stay longer."

"It's okay," she says. "Really. My mom will be back in a couple of hours anyway. I'm glad you woke up."

She gets up and wraps herself in a silky robe, running a hand through her hair. I yank my jeans on and button them and then reach for her, pulling her against me. She giggles as I kiss her neck from behind, knowing I'll probably be hard again just from her butt rubbing against the front of my jeans. She turns in my arms and loops her arms around my neck, reaching up on tiptoe to kiss me.

"I didn't even realize we fell asleep," she says.

"Me neither."

She nuzzles at the front of my shirt, and I smile, cupping the back of her head.

"I wish you didn't have to go," she said.

"I know. Me too. We can do something later, though, if you want. Since you're my girlfriend now we can hang out without having to sneak around."

She stiffens, and I realize my choice of words. Well, she can't be surprised. We're essentially dating already—I don't think joking about calling her my girlfriend is that crazy.

"Yeah. Text me," she says.

"I will."

I kiss her again and then sprint downstairs to my car, waving goodbye to where I can see her silhouette in the window. If I'm lucky, no one will even notice I was gone all night.

CHAPTER 19
lily

I watch him drive away, standing at my window. I let the sun wash over my skin and I smile as the warmth floods through my veins.

Last night was amazing. I've heard horror stories from my girlfriends about losing their virginity, but I'm beginning to think it was just because they were with the wrong person. Not that it wasn't physically uncomfortable, even painful, at least the very first time—it was. But he didn't get frustrated. He didn't act as though I were being dramatic. He waited to make sure I was okay. I don't think he knows what that meant to me.

I've never had someone care about me as much

as Jacob does. When he dropped me off last night, I immediately ached for him. It didn't matter that Rob and I had just—technically—broken up, or that I'd just seen him five minutes ago. I needed him. The fact that he needed me just as badly makes my heart ache. *Is this what it feels like to fall?* I ask myself. *Is it really so easy?*

A part of me worries I'm moving too fast. My feelings for Jacob are deepening so rapidly that I can't stop them and I can't control what's happening. I shove the thought from my mind. I don't have an answer for it anyway.

I sigh, shrugging off my robe again so I can shower. My room is lonely without him, quiet and still. There are pillows on the floor and my sheets somehow ended up at the foot of the bed in a crumpled heap. It's a mess, but I don't care. My body feels different, gilded somehow, like my edges have been dipped in gold. As I stand in front of the mirror, I look the same on the outside, but inside I can feel a glow that I know must be from his touch. I turn on the shower, wincing a little as I move. There is some pain between my legs, but it's not bad. I'm more sore after back-to-back dance classes, anyway.

That reminds me—I need to invite Jacob to the showcase. Briefly, I consider the idea, biting my lip. I want him there to watch me, but what if someone I know happens to see him there? I'm not comfortable yet with people knowing about Jacob and me. Rob and I just broke up and I still feel a little weird about the whole thing. His sisters dance in my studio though, so that's an easy excuse if someone notices him at the event.

The showcase is in a few weeks, and I've had my routine down for months, but it needs to be absolutely perfect. I bite my lip, going over my solo in my head. Briefly I remember that my black pointe shoes are part of my costume. I haven't seen them around lately, and I don't think they're in my bag. I better find them—they're perfect for the costume. I got the idea right after Jacob and I met at the convention. Everything needs to be flawless. I step into the shower, thinking of pirouettes and cabrioles, and Jacob's lips on mine.

The next few weeks streak by so quickly that I'm still not convinced I'm not dreaming. Lily and I haven't gone a day without seeing each other since the night at her house. She's been over at my house for dinner a few more times, and my parents seem to be getting used to seeing her face around our house. The twins loved her on sight; now, when she walks into my house, they each grab one of her hands and hold it until I pry them off. I went to take them to dance class and watched Lily in the advanced class the other day. I think it must have been ballet, because she had on those shoes that let her go on her tiptoes. If I thought watching Lily in real life was graceful, seeing her dance, even briefly, was a whole different story. She moved like a part of the music, her body arching and leaping and bending in ways that seem to defy basic human law. The girls were just as enraptured as I was.

Now, I'm back at the studio again to pick up Lily from ballet. She comes out to meet me in the lobby, still in her pink leotard and tights.

"Hey," she says, kissing me. "Hang on, let me grab my bag."

She tosses it over her shoulder and we head to my car, her hand in mine. She is chitchatting about the showcase, filling my ear with words, but I could listen all day.

"So, Deborah Zimmers has just confirmed she's attending, and Louisa Reyes. Those are directors of two of the biggest dance companies in the Pacific Northwest."

"Wow," I say. "That's big time."

"Yeah, it is. I need to be perfect."

"Lil," I say. "You're going to be great. Don't stress."

"I'll be calmer if I know you're watching."

"You know I'll be there. I wouldn't miss it."

She smiles at me, her eyes lighting up, and my heart cartwheels in my chest. I head downtown to Cloudburst for ice cream, wondering how to go about telling Lily I've fallen in love with her.

Lily chooses strawberry this time, and I pick rocky road like always. We find a booth and sit down. Lily has pulled sweats on but she is still wearing her leotard like a top, her hair up in her ballet bun. She eats the ice cream in tiny bites and I watch her, smiling for no reason.

"Hey, Lil," I ask. "Don't you think it's time I met your mom?"

"Huh?" She is craning her head toward the front of the store. I hear the ding of the bell as a group of people enters.

"I said—"

"Get down," hisses Lily. She grabs the back of my shirt and literally forces us down underneath the booth, ducking her head under the table.

"Lily, what the hell?"

"Shhh," she shushes me. The group I heard come into the store walks by and I hear female voices. They're laughing and talking, looking over the ice cream choices a few feet from us. Lily's hands are wrapped in handfuls of my shirt so tightly I'm afraid it's going to rip. Finally, they decide to go somewhere else and all file out. She releases me as they leave, sighing with relief. She crawls out from under the table and sits back down on the bench like nothing happened.

"Well, that was close," she says, going back to her ice cream. "What were you saying?"

"What was that about?" I ask.

"Oh." Her cheeks flush, and her eyes dart away from mine. "Those were a few friends of mine."

"So?"

"So, it's weird. Rob and I just broke up—people would freak if they knew you and I were seeing each other."

"Who gives a shit what people would think?"

"Look, it just would have been weird and awkward, okay? Don't make a big deal out of nothing."

"Are you embarrassed to be seen with me?"

"I'm not embarrassed of anything. I just didn't want to deal with them."

I just shake my head and look down at my ice cream. I can't believe she would still be worried about things that people would say about us. She plays with her ice cream, too, and I shove mine away, suddenly not hungry anymore.

CHAPTER 21
jacob

The drive home is long and silent. Lily tries to start a conversation a few times, but I answered back with one word and eventually she gave up. I'm not trying to be a dick, but I'm hurt. It doesn't exactly feel good when the woman you love tries to hide you from her friends in public. I know her and Rob broke up fairly recently, but he's an asshole, so who cares? I couldn't care less, so I don't understand what her issue is, but I don't like it. We finally reach Lily's house and she unbuckles her seatbelt, sighing. We sit quietly for another moment. I want to reach over and run my hands through her hair, kiss her goodbye, but I'm still pissed.

"Do you want to have dinner with my family?"

The question cuts through the thick tension in the car. While Lily has been to my house quite a few times by now, I've yet to meet her mother or her stepdad.

"Yeah," I say, smiling at her. "Yeah, I'd love to."

"Okay," says Lily. Her smile is a sunbeam. "Perfect. I'm busy with rehearsals right now with the showcase so close, but tomorrow night should work. Is that okay with you?"

"Yeah, that sounds fine."

"Good. I'm excited."

"Are you?" I ask.

"Yes. I've never had someone like you in my life before, Jacob, not anyone who really mattered. So I know I'm going to do weird things and make mistakes, but all I ask is that you cut me a little slack."

Her voice is direct and reasonable, but her eyes are apologizing.

"I know," I say. "I'm sorry. I'm pretty new at this, too."

"It's okay," she says, leaning in to kiss me. "We can learn together."

"Sounds good."

Lily hops out of the car.

"Can you get away tonight?" she asks. "I think the house will be open."

"If I'm not babysitting. I'll try."

"Okay."

Her smile flashes at me, and it still shocks me just how beautiful she is.

"Bye, Lil."

"Bye, Jacob."

She crosses the street and runs to her front door, blowing me a kiss before she goes inside. I head home, already wondering what to wear to dinner tomorrow. I really want to make a good impression on the woman who raised Lily. I wonder if she'll be able to tell that I'm in love with her. I wonder if she'll ask me the same thing I ask myself—why haven't I told her yet?

CHAPTER 22
lily

I can't find those stupid pointe shoes anywhere. The showcase is in a couple of days and my black pointe shoes are still missing. I don't have time to find or dye new ones. I know they're around somewhere, but now I'm starting to worry. I've looked everywhere. My room is a tornado of books and pillows and clothes, all tossed frantically at some point during the search.

My phone buzzes and it's a text from Jacob. He's supposed to be coming over in about an hour for dinner, and I'm sort of freaking out. When I asked my mom if I could bring a boy over for dinner, to meet her and my stepdad, all she did was raise an eyebrow at me and say, "That should be fine." With my mother, it's hard to say whether that's a good sign or bad.

I invited him for dinner mostly because I want him to meet my mom, but also because he was so angry about the whole ice cream parlor thing. I admit I acted a little rashly, but everything with us is still so new that it's going to take me some time to adjust. He did seem really hurt, though—he wouldn't talk to me the entire way home. Dinner will hopefully smooth things over. I don't want him thinking I don't care about him; I do. For whatever reason, that step is just a hard one for me to take. I don't want to open myself up and give people the opportunity to judge me.

I pace my room, still thinking about the shoes. My phone buzzes again and I pick it up automatically, thinking it will be Jacob.

"Hello?"

"Lily?"

My chest seizes instantly, making it painful to draw breath. Jesus Christ. It's Rob.

I immediately go to hang up, but he interjects.

"Hey, please don't hang up. Look, I'm sorry to bother you, but I found these weird looking shoes in my truck and I think they're yours."

I slap a hand to my forehead. Of course. Of course, Rob has the stupid shoes.

"I just wanted to return them to you. That's all."

My hackles are still up just from the sound of his voice, but I need my pointe shoes. I rub a hand over my face.

"Can you just drop them off?"

I don't want to have to see him, or talk to him, in person.

"Yeah. Uh, I can leave them on the front porch or something."

"Okay. Now?"

"Yeah."

That should be fine, right? It might be cutting it a little close, but Jacob still shouldn't be here by then.

"Lily, I just wanted to say I'm really sorry about what happened the day you came over here. I was totally out of line."

I trace the spot on my cheekbone where the bruise had lingered for almost two weeks.

"I know there's no excuse, but I've been taking anger management classes. I just wanted you to know that."

"Good for you," I say. It's a start, at least, for Rob.

"Thanks. Anyway, I'll be by to drop off the shoes in a few minutes. Thanks, Lily."

"Thank you for bringing them to me."

"No problem."

The line goes dead. Well. I don't care to have any sort of relationship with Rob, but I'm glad he sounds better. Maybe he's learning how to control his anger. I stuff my phone in my pocket and head downstairs to help with dinner. I'm excited to see Jacob; the thought makes me bounce on my way into the kitchen.

Ten minutes later I hear a car pull in front of the house. I look through the front window and Rob is parking on my street. He gets out of his truck and drops my black pointe shoes on the welcome mat. He glances at the front door and then turns to look across the street. I hear a voice raised, and for an instant I think Rob is yelling something before the voice strikes a less familiar cord with me. I watch as Rob's face turns dark red, and he steps into the street. What is going on? I open the front door and step outside, trying to see what's making Rob so angry. I see a familiar car parked across the street. As the driver slowly gets out, my hands go icy cold. My stomach is alive with nausea.

Jacob is standing across the street, holding a bouquet of sunflowers.

No. No, no, no.

I know what he saw—Rob's truck. He must be thinking I asked him to stop by. I start to cross the street. Jacob and Rob are already arguing, walking toward each other. I hurry to get between them. My mind is only focused on keeping them apart. That's the only thing making it through the sick feeling in my chest.

"Jacob," I say, "Stop."

"What the fuck is he doing here?"

"Me?" Rob is level with the two of us now. I'm already stepping in between the two boys, hoping to stop something before it begins.

"Yes, you, asshole. I think Lily told you pretty clearly that she wanted nothing to do with you."

"Who are you? Her fucking father?"

Rob laughs for a moment, and I look at Jacob. I've never seen him like this, his eyes are cold and glassy, and his entire body is tense, a coiled wire.

"Jacob," I say. "Please, just calm down and let me explain."

"What does she have to explain to you?" says Rob, and then realization dawns on his face. "Holy shit. It was true. You are seeing someone else."

"Yeah, she is," says Jacob, taking a step forward. His chest meets my outstretched palm.

"I knew it," growls Rob.

"What the fuck do you care?"

"She was my girlfriend—"

"Yeah, exactly. *Was.*"

"Fuck off."

"At least I treat her better than you ever did," says Jacob, pushing against my hand.

"What do you know about how I treated her?"

"I was there after she told you she wanted to break up. I saw the fucking bruise on her face."

"Jacob," I say. "Stop. Let it go."

"You think I can let something like that go? You think you can just have him over here and I'm going to be okay with that? You can't do shit like this, Lily."

The words stop my heart, and I drop my hands out of shock.

"You're just jealous because I had her first," says Rob.

"You might have had her first," says Jacob, "but she's *mine* now."

Jacob lunges forward and punches Rob in the jaw so hard I can hear the crack. I shriek, trying to pull them apart, but I just catch the edge of someone's elbow and go flying. They fall against Jacob's car with a crash. I'm helpless as Rob lands a punch against Jacob's ribs and they roll onto the concrete.

"Stop it!" I scream. It's hard for me to watch; it reminds me too much of how I felt fighting with Rob. I fight the sick waves of nausea washing over me and see an opening. I dart over and haul Jacob off of Rob, pushing him behind me. Rob scrambles up and leaps forward and I slap a hand against each of their chests.

"Lily," says Jacob, blood dripping from his lip. "Take your hand off of me."

"No," I say. Tears make it hard to speak. I didn't even know I was crying. "Stop."

My voice breaks and Jacob's eyes flicker to me.

"Stop now," I say. Rob wipes blood from under his nostril with the back of his hand. Both boys are still glowering at each other and breathing hard, but they're calm.

"Rob, leave," I say quietly, turning him. "Now."

He hesitates, looking at Jacob, and turns to walk heavily back across the street. His truck starts and he roars away in a cloud of smoke. I turn back to Jacob, who is now glaring at me.

"He just came to drop off my pointe shoes," I whisper. "You can go see—they're on the porch."

"I can't believe you let him come within a hundred yards of you."

"Jacob, it was just for the shoes. Please believe me." I am starting to panic, the words choking in my throat. Jacob's face is set and drawn, his jaw tense.

"You could've told me," he says. "You didn't have to go behind my back."

"He just called twenty minutes ago and said he had them!" I throw my hands in the air as my frustration mounts. "This wasn't premeditated to betray you."

"Is there still something going on between you two?"

I take a step back from the car, my breath caught in my throat. I don't know how to say, "No," emphatically enough in a way that will make him listen. I can't believe he would actually think that, even for a second.

"No," I say quietly. "No, Jacob. You know that."

"Seems like I don't know much," he says tightly. "I didn't know you were embarrassed to be with me. I didn't know you were still talking to Rob."

"We are not talking! We talked, for thirty seconds!"

Fury is mounting inside me at his stubbornness, and more than that at his attitude.

"You know what," I say quietly. "I can't do this."

"What?"

"I can't have someone else trying to control me. I've been there, and I got out. I'm not going back again."

"Lily, I'm nothing like him."

"I didn't think so," I say. "But now it seems like all you want to do is control my entire life, just the way he did. I won't be with someone who doesn't trust me."

Jacob looks horrified, but the stubborn mask is still there, and I know he isn't ready to back down.

"You know, Lily, you came looking for me. You were the one who started this."

"What are you talking about? What does that have to do with this?"

He has dropped the sunflowers, and the petals are scattered over our feet.

"You started this, and you made me believe you were ready for your life to change. Well, it looks like I was wrong. You're not ready to move on from who you were pretending to be the whole time we were in high school."

He is spitting the words out like they're leaving a bad taste in his mouth. I am motionless.

"I'm not two different people, Jake," I say. "Whatever lives you're talking about, they're both mine. They're both a part of who I am."

"Well, you better pick a side. I'm done playing games here."

"I don't have to do anything!"

I am yelling again, shoving at his chest with a hard slap. He looks at me as though he's never seen me before. I have never been so livid in my life—it's as if someone shoved a red-hot poker through my chest. I ball my hands into tight fists.

"You will not tell me how to live my life," I hiss. "If you don't trust me, that's your problem. Not mine. I won't cater to your insecurities and I won't listen to you berate me for something that you think I did wrong. Rob came here to drop my shoes on the front fucking porch!"

"Well, I won't be with someone who goes behind my back."

We stand there, staring at each other, and for a moment something in his eyes shifts and I think he's come back to me, but then the shield goes back up.

"Fine," I say quietly. The wind blows a strand of my hair into my eyes and I brush it away. "Fine. Then I'll make this easy for you."

I turn on my heel and walk away with quick steps, carried by anger. The tears flood my eyes and I know he can hear the sobs wracking my throat, but he doesn't follow me. I walk away from another man who wants to possess me, not be with me, and I walk away from the hard stare coming from someone I don't recognize. I don't know who Jacob is right now, but I'm never going back to someone who won't let me live my life, and who won't trust me. I scoop up my pointe shoes from the porch, and as I open the door, I hear his engine. I turn and watch his car speed off, and then the tears fall so fast that I don't see anything at all.

CHAPTER 23
jacob

It's been nearly a week since I've talked to her. I've picked up the phone a thousand times and let it fall again. I've even driven halfway to her house, twice, before turning back around. I run over every detail of what happened obsessively, over and over. I can't get her eyes out of my head, the way they pleaded with me to understand. I was too mad to see it then, but now it's all I notice.

It will be a much better idea to let the whole idea of Lily go. It was dangerous, how much I cared about her, when she definitely didn't seem to be on the same level. I had an idea it would end like this. When I saw Rob pull up to her front door, it did something to me. That was the guy who had yelled at her, who had bruised her face and made her cry so hard she couldn't catch her breath. I was there that day. I picked her up and took care of her and held her until she fell asleep in my arms. Even knowing the reason why he showed up, I couldn't handle seeing him there. She should have told me. A part of me knows that she's not the only one to blame, but my stubbornness is having a field day keeping that part of me silenced.

"Jake?" my mom's voice echoes down the staircase and I hear footsteps.

"Yeah?"

She comes in my room and looks over to where I'm sitting on my bed.

"Are you coming to the recital?"

"What recital?"

"The twins have their dance recital today. You know that—I've told you about a thousand times. It's the same one that Lily's in."

Shit. I forgot the girls were performing in the same recital as Lily. They're in the beginner's class, so they go on before her. I would skip the whole thing entirely, but I know Elizabeth and Elaina would ask where I was. They wouldn't understand. I can just go to watch them and leave before Lily goes on.

"Yeah, I'm coming. But I have to leave early."

"You're not staying for the whole thing?"

She's really asking if I'm staying to watch Lily. She knows that she hasn't been around lately, but I've made it clear that the topic is off limits.

"No," I say. "I'm not."

My mom looks at me for another second across the room, and just nods. She walks up two steps and turns back around.

"Sometimes, the people we love deserve a second chance," she says. "And you're not the only one who's hurting right now, Jake."

"I don't want to talk about this."

"I'm just saying. Consider her side a little more. I've seen her with you. She cares about you. Maybe it's time to face what happened between you two."

With that, she heads back upstairs. I bury my face in my hands.

Is she right?

I didn't consider Lily's point of view. I didn't consider the fact that Rob had tried to control her and that was the last thing she needed. It makes me sick to think that I could have done the same thing. Rob is the farthest thing from who I want to be.

I glance over at the phone screen that has been dark since I left Lily's house. She hasn't called or texted and every time I see no new messages I want to go back to that day and change everything. I would still be mad to see Rob anywhere near Lily, but maybe I overreacted. Maybe we can find a middle ground somewhere, because I know I can't live like this. I don't want to live without her.

The lights of the stage are so bright that I can't make out the faces of anyone in the audience. My mom is tugging on the laces of my costume, and I'm poking my head out of the wings, hoping that someone will turn the lights down so I can get a look at the people filing in. I'm still hoping to see his face, even though I've told myself over and over that he won't come. I was so excited to perform for Jacob, but my excitement for the night has disappeared with him. There's a hole in my chest that I can't seem to fill.

"Stand still," says my mom. "I can't lace you up when you wiggle so much."

"Sorry," I mutter. I glance in the mirror hanging on the wall. My makeup has been applied, and I don't recognize myself. My lips are dark red, my eyes fringed with thick lashes and dark eyeliner. My costume is a black leotard, lacy and long-sleeved, with black tights and my black pointe shoes creating a dark silhouette. There is a delicate tiara on my head. My piece is called "Queen of the Night," and if I can pull it off, it will be amazing. I know this even despite my feelings about Jacob. I based it on Miss Diamond and her ensemble, but I put my own twist on it that I like to think of as my own. My red cheeks and lips, the lace and the tiara—that's all me. I look powerful and mysterious and I try to focus on that.

I try not to think of the missed steps in my last practices, the way my limbs feel heavy and clumsy. Nothing has been right since that day and I'm not sure how to make it right. I know, though, that I wasn't completely in the wrong. I'll never have someone scare me or be aggressively possessive ever again. But I know Jacob isn't like that—he was angry. We both were. And I miss him. I miss him every day. Stupid, stubborn boy. How did things get so mixed up?

"Okay, Lily," says my mom. "You're all set. Break a leg."

"Love you," I say.

"Love you."

She kisses my forehead and leaves to find her seat in the audience and I'm left alone. The other dancers are all backstage; I'm waiting in the wings to go on. I wish I could summon some of the emotion that's been building up over this night for so long, but I can't. I'm a shell, completely numb. The lights dim and I can finally make out faces. There's my mom and Paul, right in front of the stage. There's the director from one of the companies I'm hoping to join.

As my eyes continue to skim over the faces, my heart stops.

Jacob is here.

I see him. Oh my god, oh my god, he's here. He's sitting in an aisle seat, his face still and serious, but he's *here*. My heart is beating so fast I'm afraid it will fly out of my chest. For the first time in days, I am alive. I'm full with the electricity that only he incites within me.

The emcee announces me and I jolt at the sound of my name and walk out onto the stage.

"Senior Dancer Lily Kingston, next, performing an original piece, titled, 'Queen of the Night.'"

I bow my head and wait for the orchestra to start my music. I am trembling from head to toe.

The lights glow, my music begins, and I start the dance. I can't see anything but the dark wood beneath my feet. Still, I can feel his eyes on me the entire time, like a caress, and he makes me better. My muscles are flexible and strong, my movements sure and smooth. I have entered a realm where I am dancing better than I thought I was capable of, with more grace and continuity of movement than I knew was possible. I am filled with light and fire, the burning inside me glowing bright as an ember. I lose track of everything but the breath in my lungs and the primal beat of the music within me.

When I finish, I hold my final pose, breathing hard, and the applause is a roar. My mother leaps to her feet, then my stepdad, and then everyone else, including the directors, I notice. I bask in the attention like a rose tilting her face toward sunshine, drinking it in, and then I take my bows and exit the stage. I am the last act; there is no reason to wait. Quickly, I remove my toe shoes and walk straight into the audience. People are starting to disperse and head home or look for their respective performer, and I edge past them, my eyes locked on the figure standing at the very back.

Jacob doesn't touch me when I finally get there, but his eyes are soft.

"Hi," I say, still breathing hard from my performance. "I didn't think you'd come."

"Well, the twins were in the recital, too."

"Oh, of course. That's why you're here."

I feel like an idiot.

There is an awkward moment of silence. I move to allow an older couple to get past me. Jacob stays still.

"You were incredible," he says. "I came for the twins, but I came for you, too."

I meet his eyes and see sparks.

"Look, Lily," says Jacob, and his voice is soft. "I'm sorry for the way I acted. Especially after the relationship you'd just ended, I had no right to attack you that way. The last thing I want is for you to feel that I want to control you, or that I don't respect you."

I stand in front of him, drinking in the flood of his apology.

"I might have been angry, but you didn't deserve the way I acted. I was just so mad about what Rob did to you—I couldn't see straight."

"I've never seen you like that," I say quietly. "But I know deep down you were hurt and worried about me. I was just afraid you'd want to take over my entire life the way he did."

"I don't want to change a thing about you or control you. Lily, I want you to feel like you can be yourself around me," says Jacob, reaching to cup my cheek in his palm. His eyes are searching mine. "That's all I want."

I take a deep breath. If there's anyone I feel safe with, it's Jacob. Even after everything, and that tells me what I need to know.

"I'm sorry, too," I say. "I didn't mean to hurt you."

"It's okay," he says, and the beginning of his smile is like a sunrise. "Really. It's okay."

I have already moved into his arms, reaching my lips up to his. It feels like an eternity has passed since I've felt his touch. He wraps his arms around me. Behind his shoulder, I see a director approach my instructor and a thrill of excitement floods my body.

"I danced for you tonight," I say to Jacob, looking up into his eyes. "I hope you know that."

"I do," he says quietly. "I'm honored."

"You make me better, Jake. I mean that. As a dancer and a person."

"I love you."

My mouth drops open, and I must look ridiculous, because Jacob starts laughing. I can't stop smiling. Later, there will be time to introduce him to my mom, time to talk with the director about my future. But in this moment, there is only Jake and me, the way it should be.

"I didn't mean to blurt it out like that," he says, grinning at me like a fool. He runs a hand through his hair. "I should have said it, I don't know—better."

"You said it perfect," I sputter. "You said it because you meant it."

"I do," he says. "I really do."

I lace my fingers with his, letting the spaces between his fingers fill the ones between mine.

"I love you, too," I say, and he kisses me, sealing the promise.